Permission To Lie

Julie Chevalier's award-winning short stories and poems have appeared in many literary journals including *The Best Australian Stories, Antipodes, Southerly,* and have been broadcast on ABC Radio National. *Women of Antiquity* 2002 was joint runner-up for the Overland Magazine Judith Wright Poetry Prize for New and Emerging Poets, 2008. Her poetry collection, *linen tough as history* is to be published by Puncher & Wattmann and *darger: his girls* won Third Prize in the Newcastle Poetry Award 2011. She lives in Sydney.

julie chevalier

permission to lie

SPINELESS WONDERS
www.shortaustralianstories.com.au

Spineless Wonders

BN01164417

PO Box U220
Strawberry Hills
New South Wales, Australia, 2012

www.shortaustralianstories.com.au

First published by Spineless Wonders 2011

Typeset in Calisto MT 11/18
Printed and bound by Lightning Source Australia.

National Library of Australia Cataloguing-in-Publication entry

Chevalier, Julie, 1939-

Permission to Lie/Julie Chevalier; illustrations by Paden Hunter.

1st ed.

9780987089700 (pbk.)

Hunter, Paden.

A823.4

Spineless Wonders is a proud member of the Small Press Underground Networking Community (SPUNC)

with gratitude and thanks
to those whose advice and encouragement
made the difference

Contents

Lies of omission

All the other journos are sandwiched together, shouting questions but he manages to remain poised.

'*Exactly* when did the developer know the site was contaminated?'

I work my way closer, jotting down Clifford Casey's answers as fast as I can.

'The safety of the builders excavating the site is my primary concern, and, it goes without saying, the concern of the Director.'

'Liar!'

A woman's harsh voice but I can't spot her in the crowd.

'Go on, admit it. Lies of omission!' Her voice again, shrill and louder. What's she on about?

He gets the final word, 'And I assure you, the Director shares your interest in the wellbeing of all the people of the City of Sydney and its environment, as well as the shareholders of this company.'

What was Casey lying about? I'm hanging around waiting for everyone to leave when a woman, too expensively dressed to be a journo, hands me the developer's propaganda. She corners Casey, talks to him while flicking a dark red fingernail toward me. She isn't telling him I yelled out 'liar' is she?

He strolls towards me, cool as.

'I see you have the press release,' he says.

'I like your tie,' I blurt out.

I'd planned to say I admired the way he managed information and then ask for an interview. I have no idea what made me say something so gauche unless it was the frames of his glasses, wire as fine as pencil lines, or his cheekbones.

Casey's carrot-coloured hair is parted on the side and he's pale. All the men work outside where I come from. I'm attracted to those who shun the sun.

'And what can I do for you?' I hear him asking.

For one second I fear that he is going to call me *young lady* but I thrust my card at him before he gets a chance, then spoil it by faltering when I notice he isn't wearing a ring. I tell him I'd like to interview him and at the same time, I have this thought that he might be going to offer me a job.

He takes his glasses off, puts them back on, looks at the card, says, 'Jacki. Good name for a journo,' and takes them off again.

'Yes.' I touch my glasses. Others are waiting to talk to him.

'You want to talk to me about … ?'

'Loyalty and the media.'

That night, I stare into the mirror at my own clunky glasses. Although I'm a lot younger than he is, I need them. All the time. None of this on again, off again business.

He has no idea how sexy he looks. Too restless to sleep, I write in my   journal, *fine frame, elegant bones, designer glasses and an Italian silk tie.*

Clifford Casey phones the next morning, willing to answer a few questions. He suggests we meet over drinks at the same hotel. He contacted me.

I get there early to find a spot where I can record, if he gives permission, but he is already sitting at the table right in the centre of the action.

'How much does every day of delay cost the developer?'

'Much less than people imagine. Owning earthmoving equipment and plant minimises overheads.'

'To gain time for the lobbyists?'

'Yes and no. Speed is essential. Consultation with stakeholders shows that minimal disruption of traffic and parking around the site is highly valued.'

'Why delay removing the contamination?'

'Technological changes are coming which will make the removal far safer in the near future.'

'What technological changes?'

'I'm not at liberty to say but take my word for it, the environmentalists will be chuffed.'

He wants to check the accuracy of what I've written so we arrange to meet again. Of course he forgets to bring the photos of the site.

I spend a whole day in the happy state of imagining and deeming these same imaginings to be absurd. I hope he is interested in me because of who I am, not just because I might be useful to him as a journalist. At the hotel he greets me by touching my arm and hands me a cocktail - creamy with a touch of ginger and the tropics. He's drinking martinis. I buy him one, while scolding myself for spending the food kitty money so frivolously. He leads me to the elevator. I tell myself he is just getting the photos of the site. We are walking down the corridor discussing art deco light fixtures, and he unlocks the door and I should just say, *hey, isn't there something we need to talk about?* but the warm room is as seductive as a florist's shop. He takes me by the hand and leads me past the big bed to a spa. Rose petals are floating on the surface.

'For you, Jacki.'

My high school teacher liked to link literature to real events. She taught me about the role of the lover and the belovèd. Some people like to pursue and some like to be pursued. Like Gatsby and Daisy. Just when I worked out that I wanted to be independent. Just when I knew that I wanted to be the one who was pursued, she started quoting another of her favourites, T. S. Eliot.

'Jacki, if you don't *force the moment to its crisis* you'll be stuck here forever.' Stuck in a rural town, the way she was.

'Go on writing your poems but apply for journalism at uni.'

Nobody back home would think of putting rose petals in a bathtub, even if the lawns were covered with rosebushes.

It's spring and the smell of jasmine lingers in the lanes at dusk. In my shared house I sit at the kitchen table next to the window to write. Satiated insects mate in the air. Birds, drunk on sunshine and inebriated insects, sing from their nests into the evening. Cats howl. I delete *moonlight* and *yearning* from my poems and drink too much beer. I promise myself he'll never see these shabby rooms. He must be aware of the difference in our lifestyles too because he never invites me to his place.

After more hotel rooms, Cliff takes me to see a furnished flat upstairs at the back of a terrace house. It's an investment or something, not the place where he lives. We'll be able to see each other more, he says, if I move in.

'It's probably some negative-gearing-tax-dodge-scheme,' my girlfriend says.

'But I want to be independent.'

'You're only young and gorgeous once. You have the rest of your life to be independent,' she says.'He can afford it.'

She and I agree that men should use condoms. It's too risky for me to have unprotected sex with him again. I should have insisted on using them at the hotel but I didn't want him thinking I was experienced and sophisticated. I move into his flat and buy condoms.

The flat overlooks a vegetable garden. An old man, Sam, gardens even when rain drips off the brim of his hat. His garden reminds me of ours back home. I can almost hear the clucking and crowing of chooks and roosters.

Cliff comes over after work a couple of times a week. I put aside my tape recorder and jump up to give him a hug when he reaches the top of the back steps. He hands me a package – white percale sheets. He's a prick if he thinks my sheets are grubby just because they're faded.

'Thanks. Choose them yourself?'

'I thought you'd like them.'

He brings takeaway meals, sets the bag of plastic boxes on

the table where I write. He rolls up his sleeves when I hand him the corkscrew. I close my laptop and get out chopsticks. I eat some of the vegetarian meal and he eats the meat one, then he finishes the rest of mine. I know he's carnivorous even if I don't know much else about him. He tells me he'll be away from Sydney for a fortnight on business.

'By yourself?' I force myself to ask.

'Some of the time.'

'You live alone?' I need to know.

'I like to spend time by myself, Jacki.'

I can see why his communication skills are so valued by the developers.

He reappears wearing a series of new shirts and co-ordinated ties.

'That tie from Italy?'

'You, of all the people I know, should go to Italy.'

'With you?'

'You'd love Florence.'

My questions freeze in the air. If he loved me, wouldn't he want to travel with me?

Things become clearer when one of the journos at the newspaper mentions Cliff Casey's wife. That explains why he never spends the night. I don't want to even think about her. I hope my parents haven't heard anything.

I buy a moleskin notebook to write in while I wait for him at the top of the back stairs. I'm trying to find a metaphor for our relationship. I even Google Donne's twin compasses. I'm the constant compass point. Cliff moves around and comes back. A metaphor like that. Pity Donne thought of it first. Sam goes into his shed at dusk just before I spot Cliff, carrying a briefcase as well as the takeaway.

'Take off the glasses, please,' he says as soon as we're inside, reaching his hand up towards them, 'I'm going to take your picture.'

'No and no. I can't see without them.'

'I've brought the camera and champagne, to celebrate that the red in your hair has finally grown out.'

'As if.' I dyed it green when I started uni. Time for green again. He can take the champagne home to her.

'Will you take the studs out?'

'Fuck off.'

'I'll use a soft focus so the holes won't show.'

'Why are you doing this, Cliff?'

'I like to look at you.'

'Not the real me, you don't.'

Sometimes it's hard to feel beloved. Mum and Dad want a snapshot of me looking like Miss Regional Ag Show in the hand-knitted jumper Mum sent but I'm not compromising who I am for them either.

We take the plates into the living room so we can eat in comfy chairs. I have deliberately left the cabinet doors open. I hope Cliff will tell me about the miniatures and the sand trays stored inside. The miniatures are grouped on the shelves by subject – farm animals, archetypal heroes, families, weapons, vehicles. I wonder how anyone could have abandoned them, like leaving poems behind. He turns his chair so he's facing away from the cabinet.

'What are the miniatures for?'

'Some wanky, psychotherapy thing.'

'What's it called?'

'Sand play.'

'Who lived here?'

He looks out the window.

Later I Google, Sandplay. *Jungian therapists in Zurich ... use figures to enact personal dramas ... like dream therapy.* The woman who called Cliff a liar at the media conference didn't seem dreamy.

Cliff pours the last drops of wine into our glasses before we go to the bedroom. Does his wife have dinner waiting when he arrives home late or does he pick up a second order of takeaway?

My friends envy my flat, takeaway meals and freedom. Everyone wants to go out every night and have sex and no one wants to get tied down. I've just opened Neruda's love poems that I got from the library. *I want/To do with you what spring does with the cherry trees.* I'm waiting for Cliff to say something like that.

On Saturday night, when my girlfriend stops at my place before we go up to the pub, she says, 'Forget the fairy floss trees, read Dorothy Porter if you want to feel *full of trapped bubbles/like honeycomb.*' She says not practising safe sex is refusing to accept adult responsibilities. Bloody feminists and their unrealistic expectations. I can't convince Cliff to use one, let alone buy them. To change the subject I show her the miniatures. She picks up the guitar, the beer bottle and the panel van. She moves a man and a woman to opposite sides of a mirror estuary and buries something in the sand. After she leaves I take the packet of condoms from the bureau drawer and place it on top.

The next time I toss Cliff the packet in what I hope is a playful manner. He places them on the floor.

'I've been married for years and never … '

'I'd prefer not to use them too, but.' I dive for the floor, grab the packet, open it, tip out condoms, tear the foil with my teeth, and hand him one.

'We're doing OK without, Jacki.'

'Too risky.'

'Don't you trust me? You're telling me to have a test?' He crosses his arms.

'I'm asking you to use a condom.'

'Trust me.'

Even if I wanted to, I don't have time to find somebody else to go out with. There is never enough time for writing. I write curled up in an armchair, on the bus, in a library, a coffee shop, even in the bathtub. Knees can be islands.

My period is a month overdue before I tell him. I'm afraid I'll never see him again.

'If I'm pregnant, you'll pay for the abortion and come with me, won't you?'

'I don't believe in abortion.'

'What the fuck?' He must be in favour of abortion if he's so bloody arrogant about contraception.

'I don't believe in killing living creatures.'

'Your wife?'

'She doesn't believe in killing living creatures either.'

'That's not what I meant and you know it.'

I should have asked him straight out what would happen to me and the baby. If there were one. But I hate messing up the time we have together by arguing. I have only myself to blame. Cliff shouldn't have brought beer as well as wine and we shouldn't have drunk so much.

I ring up my girlfriend when I finally get my period. I am so relieved I don't have to have an abortion or face my parents, I vow never to have unprotected sex again and make an appointment with her GP to get the pill as well, even though I hate the idea of pumping my body full of horse piss.

Clarissa Casey rings me at work. Before I know what's happening, I have agreed to meet her for coffee on Saturday.

As I near the cafe I try to imagine I am a worldly mistress having coffee with a wronged wife in a French film. The momentary distraction ceases when I am unable to jam myself into the role of worldly mistress. I am a guilty girl from a small town in the country, a small town with a big church. I should have cancelled or just stood her up. I should have the guts to tell Cliff Casey I never want to see him again. Easier said!

As I check out an escape route, Clarissa beckons. Maybe she doesn't know anything. Maybe she wants to talk about something entirely different.

Almost every seat in the café is taken. I stare at her manicured hands when we order skinny lattes, then glance down at my own bitten nails. She definitely is the one with the talons.

'You were at the media conference when I met Cliff.' I give myself credit for being able to mention his name.

Clarissa nods and describes the trouble she's had finding a parking spot and finding the right coins for the meter. Someone watching would assume we knew each other. She redraws her mouth with maroon lipstick that clashes with her chartreuse top, then leans forward, pointing to a shop across the road. She lowers her voice and mentions friends who buy organic fruit and vegetables for their toddlers. Why is she whispering this yuppie shit? I want to avoid intimacy.

'I know everything,' Clarissa says, keeping her voice low and scraping her chair as she moves it closer to mine.

'My work often intersects with Cliff's, that's all.' I don't care if every trendy person in the café hears me

'I know about the baby.'

'Shhh! What baby?'

She must have discovered something. He hadn't told her I was pregnant, had he? He knew I wasn't.

'Look, I don't want…' I blurt out. The problem is I'm not sure exactly how much I don't want.

She orders another coffee.

'I understand perfectly,' she says.

I don't know what she understands but I know they are a team and I am an outsider.

'You pointed me out to him.'

'Cliff lets me choose.'

I blame myself for getting into this mess. Crazy Sydney. Making love to a married man with his wife's consent? Is there any weirder situation?

Is there a job going on the newspaper back home? I picture myself in a few years' time, married to a stock and station agent, covering boring weddings and fund raising events. Someone clears our table.

'I'll drop you off,' Clarissa says.

I am shivering in her car when I tell her the name of the street where I live. She drives there without needing directions, and parks. I feel used, dirty, frozen, unable to act. She waits for me to get out, then locks the doors with one sinister click. As she follows me up the stairs to my flat, she calls out, 'Your garden looks better than ever, Sam.'

They know each other. I unlock the door and she follows me into the kitchenette. I go into the bathroom and lock the door, to get a few seconds to figure out how to get rid of her. By the time I come out, she's standing next to the lounge, clutching three miniatures. I remember closing the cabinet doors.

'You don't mind?' she asks, nodding toward one of the sand trays.

'You've done this before?'

'This is my flat. Surely you know that?'

Had she been living here before I moved in or had there been others? She drips water into the sand, rakes it into landscaped terraces, smooths a track and stands two female figures on the top of the highest hill and brushes the sand off her long fingers. Her dark hair, cut blunt at her jaw line, leaves her neck exposed, as fragile as a stem. I feel like breaking it. She picks up a figure of a baby.

'I want you to have Cliff's baby for me.'

'Get out.'

At the time the rooster would crow, I get out of bed and go into the living room and stand by the trays. The figure of a woman strides across vast paddocks. Figures stand behind and in the distance ahead but she strides alone. I drag my suitcase out from under the bed and open the train timetable.

PERMISSION TO LIE

Thunder

Clifford Casey sits at the best table on the ground floor of a hotel near his office. Today, it's just drinks with a developer. Insulated by air-conditioning and plate glass, they watch the heat rise from the Sydney CBD streets as commuters rush to catch buses before the southerly hits. The developer has picked up the tab for three rounds in a row, entitling him to rave on like he's bought the drive-time broadcaster's slot.

'Here's the thing, Cliff. Say we're planning a resort on an island in Queensland. We strike shit.'

Cliff Casey is sure of two things: it pays to be lavish with romantic gestures, and generous with money. What could be easier than paying Room Service to scatter rose petals on warm water? Nothing. He's never met a woman, even Jacki, who hasn't been willing to lower her knickers for the petals of roses floating in a spa. And she's a journalist.

The developer flicks his tie to dislodge a crumb. Cliff brushes the sleeve of his third best suit. The developer grabs another handful of nuts.

'And you're called to the site. If you take the wife with you – Clarissa, right? – well, a bit on the side's not an option.'

Cliff nods. He likes his job. Likes the creative challenge of spin.

'But if you're there on your own, sex doesn't count,' the developer continues. 'Like fucking on set doesn't count. Like when the diggers were overseas or a match's played away from home.'

'Say your wife's at a conference on her own, you wouldn't mind … ?'

'Hell, yes,' says the developer, spraying more crumbs. 'Women can go without, easy. Only blokes need it every day and only a loser would pay.'

'My shout.' Cliff glances at his watch, no rush, and tries to catch the waiter's eye. He removes his glasses and touches the thin bridge of his nose.

A waiter leaves another bowl of nuts and collects the empty glasses. With long pale fingers Cliff selects three almonds, then orders a dozen oysters. Might as well hang around until the traffic clears. No napkin to wipe his hands on. Typical. No one shares his attention to detail. Except Clarissa. Cliff replaces his specs and picks up an oyster, squeezes a few drops of lemon juice on it, tips his head back, stops, looks at a chip of shell on the flesh, two chips. Cliff sends the oysters back.

'Fucking hell, Cliff. It's only shell.'

'It's not a fish and chip shop. Yeah, paying ruins the fun. Women should be lining up for it.'

'Hell, they should be paying us.'

'Apologies, Mr Casey.'

'Thanks.' He looks again for something to wipe his hands on, holds the fingers of his right hand out awkwardly in front of him as he walks to the bar and helps himself to a handful of napkins that aren't cloth, much less linen. He'll have to speak to the manager.

His grandmother used to inspect his hands. She said that with fingers like his he could be a concert pianist. She talked about insuring them, if he practised. Well, success comes in unexpected forms. His salary is proof he's the best media liaison person in property development but there's more to life than work. Sometimes.

The developer rubs his hands together, scattering salt crystals like dandruff. Cliff is looking at the next table, trying to work out which of the women reeks of cheap rose scent, an almost rancid smell. He likes the way rose petals can float on water, obscuring everything beneath. Under the surface a penis can be quiescent, sensitive to the slightest ripple or vigilant, ready to take control.

The developer is practically wringing the oyster shell to extract the last salty drop.

'Nothin' like 'em.' He smacks his fleshy lips.

Cliff agrees. 'We've just crawled out of the primordial brine ourselves. To oysters and fucking.' He raises his glass.

'To fucking oysters.'

Cliff orders another dozen. Wallis Lake ones this time. He never thought he'd replace a Baby Grand with an iMac, but Macs are the only keyboard he's played for over a decade. Maybe if he had the latest technology he would do something creative. Time to update the digital camera. Picking up these tiny cameras isn't as satisfying as hefting his old SLR Nikon with the manual override but it's light enough to carry around in a briefcase. Jacki refused to pose for him.

He picks out the plumpest oyster. No chips. Fresh as sea spray hitting the back of his throat.

Back home Cliff steps out of the shower, rubs his body with a towel the shade of the stone floor. His bedroom feels as humid as the bathroom. Moisture fogs the wardrobe doors blurring the reflected lights from the harbour. He flips on the overhead fan. Clarissa's bedroom is air-conditioned. He heaves the towel in the direction of his bathroom as though it will fly back to the chrome rod by itself. It lands in the doorway. In a flash of lightning he sees the taupe bedding. Once she must have equated taupe with masculinity. He laughs. Cliff no longer lusts for Clarissa, any more than he lusts for granite, glass and stainless interiors. Since her hysterectomy, he can't even get it up with her. Spontaneity? Lust? So long ago he can hardly remember. He never had a problem with Jacki; Clarissa pushed him into that. Her baby thing.

He remembers the morning he bit into a steamed pork bun, the rich brown sauce squirting and splattering down his chin. It must have been the first Saturday morning he spent with Jacki, about this time last year, when she'd just moved into Clarissa's old flat. He had picked up yum cha – prawns curled up like miniature infants on squares of green capsicum. She held spears of Chinese broccoli for him to nibble. He licked his fingers clean after he'd broken a chopstick trying to divide each steamed bun. Needlessly it turned out. He'd never heard of a country girl refusing to eat meat. He'd never thought to ask why.

Thunder. He unplugs the laptop on the table, stretches his arms out in front of him, thumbs low, together, while the fingers crouch into shapes that clench and unclench. Hot air rolls high over the roof, over the roof garden and further down still, toward the park and harbour. Both hands grasp at the air. God he misses Jacki's breasts, just big enough to grab hold of. He remembers the studs she continued to wear even when she knew they made her look cheap, the outrageous frames of her glasses, the gaudy green and red clothes that clashed with her awful red hair. He sees people on the street that resemble her, until they turn around.

By the time he gets to bed one of his hands is already clutching his penis. Jacki had vacated the flat without leaving a forwarding address. Her work won't say if she's coming back and she hasn't returned messages in months. Must be hiding somewhere, maybe Bondi. Unless she's gone back to her parents' property, wherever that is.

Another thunderclap; he pictures each rolling, grumbling nimbus, imagines them head-butting each other. He longs to be a school boy again, head-butting kids on the playground, knocking them over, punching their feisty fists and feet, bloodying their noses, clearing the air.

On that last night, he'd brought takeaway to the flat as usual.

'Sweet and sour? Fuck. I can't believe this. The sophisticated Clifford Casey. You can get this clichéd crap in any country town in New South Wales.'

He was fairly sure it wasn't the food making Jacki mad.

'There must be thirty decent takeaways within a kilometre.'

He'd bought takeaway from most of them. Neither Clarissa nor Jacki cooked. Did the women he was attracted to lack sensuality? Or did he only appeal to unsensual women? Or was he too quick in offering to pick up takeaway?

When he thought about Jacki he smelled the sea, like the rich piss of pied cormorants he remembered from the beach playground under Norfolk Island Pines when he was a kid.

He had wanted to crash into her, pound until he was spent. He was sick of having to pull himself to the surface, think about whether he was too rough, whether she'd come yet, whether she'd come enough times. He was tired of negotiating, tired of domestic trade-offs, tired of worrying about fertility. He envied animals.

The rain bashes on the windows. Knots of thunder somersault across the sky, faster, faster, faster. There. His gut unclenches and the rain falls slowly and steadily without interruption. He reaches for a handkerchief.

What the hell had she been so angry about?

'This isn't working for me, Cliff.'

He supposes he should have asked her what wasn't working but he was fed up with interrogation, tired of covering up. Why can't women just shut up and get on with it? She said she wasn't pregnant, but how was he to know? They hadn't used anything. He remembers wanting a baby the way he'd wanted to be a pianist.

Clarissa is out somewhere in this weather, at some art function that probably ended hours ago. He leans his face between his knees, conjuring Jacki's breasts. He should find a hooker. Someone he could really fuck.

Skim flat white

Monday night

A young, redheaded woman in thick glasses was sitting on the bench where I catch the bus to the CBD. Right where I used to sit. She stared at me, took out a black notebook just like this one, and started writing. It's hard enough having to go back to a place where you used to work without being displaced at your own bus stop as well.

A woman who's probably fifty – older than me anyway – and a schoolboy, arrived next. The woman instructed the boy to stand at the kerb where the bus was supposed to stop. I stood behind him looking at his hair as he stepped up onto the bus. It was standing like grass too new to mow. I resisted reaching up and running my hand across the top. Just as I had my foot on the step, ready to drop my ticket into the machine, the woman stepped in front of me. On purpose? The bitch. Maybe she was worried I'd take the seat next to her boy. They huddled together up the front. I took a seat facing the aisle, next to the redhead, so I could hear what they said.

Everyone at the office ignored me. I'd forgotten how stuffy an overheated office block could be. I hope the Managing Director didn't notice how many times I took off my jacket. If only menopause was a continuous power surge.

Tuesday night

OK so here I am, wasting time writing in this stupid notebook when there is absolutely nothing to say. *Write about the ways change affects you*, the vocational officer told me. All that comes to mind is that going back to my old job is easier than keeping a notebook about changing jobs, even if Graeme picked the new computer still in its box off my workstation and carried it into his plush office. He left me with a runt from the side of the road, along with a coffee stained mouse and a peeling mouse pad. *Write about how you cope.*

Wednesday night
The woman on the bus was wearing a bossy hound's-tooth suit with black and white accessories. I added paper doll tabs at her shoulders, head, wrists and ankles and substituted a yellow hat, bag and shoes. The least I could do to make up for thinking she was a bitch when I was so uptight on Monday. Probably she elbowed me by mistake. The buttery yellow looked softer and suited her tinted hair. I'd dress so the boy would be proud to be seen with me if he were mine.

Donald – I call him Donald – looked fragile, bloodless, like nothing tied him to the earth except the gaze of the woman. Maybe he was sick with cancer or something, or grieving. His eyes were shiny but his jaw was tight. Whatever the tie with her was, it was strong.

The vocational officer says I can't get redundancy for going through a normal life process.

Thursday night
Finally, a reasonable day. The worst thing I did was order mud cake for our morning tea. How was I supposed to know Graeme hated chocolate?

Friday night
The best day yet. My barista recognised me across the plaza.

'Hey! Skim Flat White! Where you been?'

I begged him to set up a street stall in the suburbs two years ago. Of course he remembers me – flattery and speed are a street stall barista's core business. Using fluted paper cups and Illy beans helps, but it's his ability to make friends that sells the coffee. The people you meet through work can fill your whole life.

Monday night
My clothes wouldn't look out of place if the graphic arts girls weren't flaunting cleavage and legs up to their knickers. Cross fingers David Jones has something that isn't too fitted. Pity to waste time and money shopping for work clothes if there's a chance of redundancy but I can't have people suspecting I'm past my use-by date. Oops. Don't know what the vocational lady will make of Merlot stains.

Monday night
Finally Loretta was at the bus stop, eager to fill me in on the goss.

'So you think life here freezes just 'cause you were transferred to suburbia?'

I strained over her head, watching for a bus to come down the hill. She was too busy telling me her news to notice The Spy peering around as though everything was out of focus, then writing in her notebook. She needs to have her thick lenses checked.

Wednesday night
Wrote fiction for the vocational officer. Sent ten e-mails and three faxes to Salaries to get my pay redirected. The man who answered the phone said the clerk who does mine is still on stress leave.

Monday night
The new people at the bus stop ignored me as usual. Loretta referred to the redhead with the glasses and laptop as 'Jacki'. I'm certain Loretta doesn't suspect Jacki is a Spy.

Had the worst bus driver this morning – a passenger fell over in the aisle. Then a young woman carrying a newspaper gave her seat to an old Asian woman. That's the second time she's given up her seat this fortnight. She must feel guilty about leaving her kid at childcare or something.

Someone sitting behind me murmured about how nice it was to be offered a seat when she was pregnant.

Thirty-four years of periods and no kid to show for it. A total waste.

* Buy tampons and iron pills.

Tuesday night

I don't call him Donald to his face. She started to tuck the label in at the back of her neck and he reached over and did it. Maybe she isn't his mother. His hand lingering on her neck made me squirm but maybe it's just me, not being accustomed to kids. Hardly any kids catch this bus. If she's fifty and he's thirteen, she'd have been about thirty-seven, old enough to know she might not have had another chance.

What makes the woman stare at him like that? Why escort him to high school anyway? Have they been threatened? They gazed into each others' eyes. The Spy's writing sounded agitated.

The vocational bitch gave me *The Big Issue* to read on the bus. She must have retrieved it from the bin while I was in the loo.

Friday night

Like all Catholics, Loretta is obsessed with wedding rings, unwed mothers and adoption but I think very few children the boy's age were adopted out. I'm so used to looking out of the left window on the trip into the city I haven't noticed the *For Sale* signs at Preterm and now they look as though they've been weathering for months. Doctors have been performing abortions there since before the boy was born.

In November, about fifteen years ago, three Indian mynah birds were diving at an overturned cicada on the pavement. The greengrocer was racing its legs in the air like it was bicycling upside down. I turned it over and I had the distinct impression it watched me as I set it on the grass and covered it with leaves to keep it hidden. I stayed with it until the birds flew away. Little things I've done right.

A fourteen year old would be in Year 9.

Wednesday night
Loretta thinks the boy has been in care and now that they're reunited, the mother and boy are trying to be perfect for each other.

'I bet he sings like an angel,' she whispered.

She keeps offering me her old Mills and Boons 'to brighten my day'. Wish she read detective novels.

Tuesday night
The woman on the bus pulled up Donald's socks, touched his peaked cap, the pin near the crest on his jacket and then the knot of his tie.

The man opposite was reading music and tapping his finger. The Spy watched the muso's lips move. He was wearing a suit instead of his usual pants and jacket. Maybe he was going to a concert after work, maybe out to dinner before, with someone special. Lucky him. Lucky person he's going out with. It's been years since a man asked me out. The muso should wear a red tie instead of a tan one with that suit. Maybe I'll mention it the next time. It never hurts to offer advice, like I told the clerical assistant at work her new hair colour gives her skin a greenish cast.

Thursday night
The woman got a seat, then cocked her head like a pigeon and looked at the floor when the bus driver yelled, 'Move up the back please.' Everyone standing shuffled back except the boy. When the shuffling stopped and he hadn't moved, she nodded approval. She wants him for herself.

I'd have chosen a popular name for my child. Like Jack, Tommy, Andy, Sally or Lucy. Names kids on playgrounds would call out to their friends.

You have to pick just the right name for each character too. Like Donald. I have a soft centre for Dad's name but no one would name a boy Donald these days.

Friday night
Donny sat between the Spy and the woman on the three fold-up seats. His right hand on his thigh. The mother's hand with its frosted nails covered his. No wedding ring. When I saw her little finger and thumb touching his pale bare skin I wanted to rush over and wedge myself between them. I wanted to rip her hand away. I watched for the tiniest sign of adolescent rebellion but instead he placed his other hand on top of hers.

The Spy's pen nib was digging into the paper. They must recognise her. How could they not notice someone with dyed Raggedy Ann hair wearing green leopard skin? She can't be writing about fashion.

I asked Loretta if she remembered the game where we made a stack of hands, drew out the bottom hand and slapped it on the top of the stack? After dinner, my family would remain around the kitchen table under the hanging lamp, the heat from the oven still warming the room. I never came home to a dark house in those days. The game only ended when the stack of hands toppled sideways and we laughed until we toppled sideways. Loretta knew. Her family still plays it.

Monday night
Cleanskins aren't bad for the price.

Tuesday night
Not even Loretta was on the bus. My fault for missing the early one. God, I'm exhausted.

'Saw you hurrying this way, Skim Flat White.' My barista hands me the cup with the straight line over the S on the lid at 8.55.

He is such a spunk, singling me out of everyone in the plaza.

After she read some of my notebook, the vocational lady told me to treat myself to an iPod for settling back into my old job so well.

French champers is definitely creamier than Omni.

Wednesday night
The woman and the boy were chatting as they took seats behind me.

'Don't worry. Mumsie'll be at the gates at 3.15.'

Mumsie! I shouldn't eavesdrop, but I'm almost certain. Donald doesn't have the clear pure voice I imagined but a westie nasal twang. He sounded nothing like a private school boy. Loretta will be so disappointed. They got off at Wynyard and walked back up George Street holding hands. They kissed on the lips – yuck – before he merged into a crowd of uniforms.

Haven't seen The Spy in yonks.

Thursday night
The vocational bitch had her little chat with Graeme. Regardless of what he said, I'm not going to counselling unless it gets me a payout.

* Buy bread roll
long life skim milk
Krispy Kremes – coupon for second dozen
chocolate x 7
remember tweezers to clean computer mouse.

Thursday night
A whole week has flown the coop. The school holidays are nearly over and the woman, the boy and the Spy have disappeared. Maybe Loretta was right and the woman has fallen for an antique dealer and the boy is boarding at a posh Southern Highlands school during the honeymoon.

The students on the bus are wearing winter uniforms now. Their noise got to me, maybe because I was tired. Near Town

Hall, one group of Year 9 girls giggled for five minutes about the word beret. Each rolled it around in her mouth and tried to pronounce it before the next one had a go, like they were tasting fine chocolate and comparing notes.

I love knowing the chocolates will be right where I left them. Pathetic really. I love being single. I'm not showing this to the vocational bitch.

Monday night

Caught the early bus. Loretta said she hadn't seen the woman, the boy or the spiky redhead. She thought Donald might be touring with his school's choir. I couldn't think of a way to break the news about his voice. Just before Wynyard, through the bus window, I saw the Spy slam the door of a cab and rush down George Street and I shouldn't have been rude to Loretta, hurrying off the bus without any explanation like that, but I was afraid I'd lose sight of the Spy. Did I run! All day I imagined Loretta's voice in my head, *I thought you were making up stories about people on the bus for a hoot!* It's all right for her.

The Spy hurried toward the arcade, lop-sided with one shoulder weighed down by an old laptop bag. I ran as fast as I could in my damned heels, across George Street but lost sight of her, finally spotted her bottle-red hair in the coffee shop about half way along the arcade, typing something on her laptop, so big it covered half the table. I hesitated outside the shop, tugged my collar back into place. The Spy pulled the lid down as I approached, turned, almost knocked it off the table and stared straight at me, her eyes magnified by the glasses.

'You can't have my characters.'

Tuesday morning

* Apologise to Loretta. Keep Donald's accent to myself.

Cherry pie

Graeme the boss keeps coming in and interrupting don't touch anything I can smell when you've been cleaning in my office Maria don't move anything but how can I clean without moving things and he say don't leave strings from the mop on the parquetry I use that mop special so's not to disturb and don't touch the confidential file drawers or the computer I don't tell him how to do his job how can I ignore the ring ringing like I call Tessa my sister and she not answer if her lover there and I not know if they out partying or asleep or dead at the side of the road so months ago I answer Graeme's phone although I be in a hurry to get away Friday he never lets me start til four and this voice say tell him I'm through with his heater and he should pick it up next weekend not this weekend so I write that down like an admin assistant they don't call 'em clericals anymore but they still call us cleaners and hand it to him and picks up the glass cleaner and he yells at me I told you not to answer the phone and I want to squirt his bald head and polish it with the cleaning rag if he weren't so cheap he'd pay for me to clean at night he says don't smoke while using aerosols and don't leave lint from the rags when you wipe the stains the coffee mugs the mug doesn't know what coffee is drinking International Roast and although Managing Director's on his door he has a fat computer waddling across the desk not like the companies upstairs with skinny screens leaving lotsa space to dust I was disinfecting his phone so a course I answer when the lady whispers I write Francesca wants you to pick up the cherry pie this weekend not next weekend and she giggles like her with the earrings who used to work upstairs and he swears and hopes I'm taking my holidays soon not waiting for Christmas and I say how you can loan someone a cherry pie and pick it up later he say don't squirt that near the aquarium you'll poison my goldfish and confidential papers including notes go through the shredder not the recycling loose lips sink ships and Graeme say get out of here right now Maria I mean it this is urgent for the Head of the Board and he marches off and this time the lady says she'd be waiting for him to bring a banana next weekend not this weekend and that's too rude to write down so I don't he's up to no good with his flippin banana but he musta taken it over there cause come the next Monday he's angry as a fireman caught with the petrol tin on his motorcycle and a match in his hand if you insist on answering my phone write exact messages and repeat back to double check and I had to pay two mortgage payments in one month cause I lose so much sleep drinking coffee and worrying I forget to pay I use paper towels on the glass-front cabinets instead of rags and he thinks I need glasses because the paper left more lint but one of the admin assistants'll do a search for a lintless cleaning cloth in fact he says I'll tell Human Resources that'd be a good interview question and Francesca who sounds like the lady upstairs who used to ask how the goldfish were keeping has some gelignite she has borrowed from him and she wants him to pick it up next weekend not this weekend and I'm askin how she's keepin and he walks in and hears me telling her take care with that jelly it might explode he tells me to mind my own business I want to mind my own business hire others to clean the offices refugees would do Afghanis even and next time Francesca rings I could ask if she needed a job and she could give him the messages in person but next she says to tell him to come over so she can return the hot chillies this weekend not next weekend and I tell her I doubt he'll want chillies on Bedarra Island when his wife's paying for the candlelight and the oysters in their shells on their beds of ice and Francesca she tells me to mind my own business and she'll give him his cold mashed potatoes back next weekend not this weekend and he tells me I'm risking my job interfering like this and buggers off and then the phone rings and I can't just let it ring she's sobbing he can pick up his ashes straight away she's finished with them.

Recycling

To welcome me to the team, Genevieve – Senior Manager, Product Design & Production – brought in special coffee, and almond croissants from Bourke Street Patisserie.

'Most travelled coffee in the world again?' asked Hal, the Senior Engineer attached to our team. In his fifties, probably. Older than the others. Hemp shirt. Faded.

'An Arabica blend from Ethiopia, Kenya and Mexico,' she said. 'You know a better one?'

'Only if you care about our carbon footprint.'

'Did you see that cartoon in the Herald about the coffee with Frequent Flyer Points?' asked Monica, the statistician in specs.

'Coffee grown in Coffs Harbour is probably good enough for people who add milk,' said Genevieve, 'but people who drink it black need the best. Sandra appreciates good coffee, don't you?'

I sipped and smiled. She had chosen me. I owed her loyalty. I wanted to look as smart as she did, but my own age, of course.

The next day, when she had flown somewhere for a meeting, Monica, Hal, and I had mugs of his organic tea. Monica told me I'd impressed Genevieve.

'You'd have thought Stina Kovacs was a shoo-in with a PhD in Environmental Studies, five years' industry experience, and project management. She, Hal and I were all here when Gen took over last year.'

'Why didn't Stina get the job?' While I was waiting to be interviewed I'd fantasised what it would be like to work under high ceilings, with everything reflected in glass and chrome. I tried to figure out how water was recycled in the hanging fountain. I was too green and yet not green enough to imagine myself in such a high tech environment.

'She'd begun another doctorate. Environmental Engineering. That would have gone against her.'

'And looking blokey didn't help,' said Hal.

'Good God.' I only had a Bachelors Degree. Thank goodness it was Science. And Honours.

'Gen likes attractive young people, like you Sandra. The image she wants for Emerald Sustainability.'

So much to have to live up to. They said Gen believed in stylish design. What Emerald's products looked like was more important than how much energy they saved. We now employed more designers than engineers. Back at my work station I googled the letters on the post-it note stuck to Hal's screen. Snafu: Situation Normal All Fucked Up.

After work on Friday Genevieve invited me to go to a new wine bar in a lane.

'Like the wine bars in Melbourne. I want you to call me Gen, now that we're friends,' she said.

She trusted me to take minutes at the team meeting. Monica e-mailed the pro forma.

Under New Business, Gen announced, 'The engineering section has to be restructured which means the Senior Engineer's position must be readvertised.'

Hal stared at his Birkenstocks.

'I'd like everyone to suggest ways Hal can improve his chances of winning his job back,' she said.

What a strange concept: winning your own job back. When my turn came I said, 'I've only just met you, Hal, but I look forward to ...'

'Cut to the chase, Sandra. How can he be more efficient?'

'Sandee's too nice,' Biliyana the accountant said, as she took her second glazed donut from the oval tray. Gen glared at her so I didn't dare take one. Later Biliyana asked where I lived and offered me lifts to work.

'Each person must be able to identify and articulate team weaknesses. Exactly what must Hal improve on?'

Monica rescued me, 'Hey Hal, have you thought about enrolling in SAMSI? The team needs someone besides me who can analyse environmental stats and do mathematical modelling.'

'And,' Gen interrupted, 'stop allocating work to backyard contractors, and contract to the big boys. They may charge too much but they have the contacts in government to get the work done fast.'

I hoped my minutes were tactful: 'Team discussion offering assistance to a colleague before he reapplies for his job.' As soon as I sent them, Gen e-mailed me back the pro forma she preferred and came over.

'No need for a pity party just because he's a greenie who's clocked on for fifteen years,' she said, handing back my minutes. 'Emerald's core business is making money. Don't say, "his job". Bullet point every criticism and suggestion.' The tone of her voice changed. 'Minutes can be used as court evidence, but people past their use-by date usually fade away quietly.' She stood behind me, staring at my screen. 'Come into the office when you're finished.'

Gold-framed prints of rainforests covered the plum walls. Air con hummed. She looked model-elegant in stilettos when she handed me a gift-wrapped parcel.

'For working back so often.'

An enamelled butterfly the size of an artificial fingernail that matched the turquoise of the blouse I'd worn to the interview. Someone should have told me then that even in the rainforest butterflies only live for three days. Hal had worked back too. She asked me to send him in. When I'd run into him in the plaza, he told me the interview committee hadn't given him one minute to speak about his work. We'd briefly swapped mobiles and entered each other's numbers.

The sound track began as he left her office.

'You have only yourself to blame,' she said. 'Don't forget to turn in your photo ID and swipe card.'

The scissors she'd been using clanked onto the desk as Gen wiped her hands against each other.

Roy, a gym junkie in a uniform, appeared next to Hal's desk. Staff who were leaving were not given the opportunity to sabotage the team's work. Roy scrutinised everything Hal put into a carton.

'Blackberry?'

'Haven't been here long enough, have I?'

'iPhone?'

'Haven't been here long enough, have I?'

Poor Hal. I doodled handcuffs. The rest of the team typed furiously. I respected him because he really lived his beliefs. A vegetarian who cycled to work. No farewell lunch. No token to mark fifteen years of service. I was a coward, staying at my desk instead of standing beside him.

Gen came out of her office tapping phone buttons. She must have heard some good news because she looked more smug than upset. She glanced at my face, then instantly parodied woe.

In October, Nan died in hospital at Port Macquarie and I told Gen I'd just hired a car to drive north to be with my family.

'You'll have to fly back from Port Skanky,' she had said. 'I need you here Thursday, crack of dawn.'

'The funeral is Friday, and Port Macquarie is not skanky.'

She looked at my face.

'Sorry about your grandmother. Port's okay. I had a decent fuck in a motel there once. But Sandra, decide if you're part of the solution here, or part of the problem.'

An opportunity to get out of the building, even if it was only to walk three blocks to a meeting, was a treat. The rectangle of November blue between the tall buildings was only marred by a few clouds. I assumed Gen would prefer walking too. She looked toned, as though she spent a lot of time at a gym. She frowned at my lace-up shoes, walked past the company Prius in the car park and slid into the passenger seat of her yellow Celica.

'You can drive. Drop me at the front so I'm not late. Then bring the car back here.' She flicked her blow-dried hair.

'But I've prepared a presentation. It even has a name. The Shower Butler.'

'Just give me the folder and I'll talk about our project. I wanted to see you away from the others because I want you to join me and a few other friends at Newport for Christmas lunch. I'm booking a beach house.'

While I ignored the request for the folder and navigated the Sydney traffic, she talked Möet, oysters, lobster. I was so gobsmacked I didn't state clearly that I wanted to present my ideas and be there for the discussion. What was I, her fucking chauffeur?

'Sorry, I go home for Christmas.'

'My friends are important contacts. Worth knowing.'

I didn't say anything when she picked up my presentation folder from the back seat. Too much was going on and it was hard to resist her offer to introduce me to good connections. But Christmas was Christmas and I was spending it with my family. I intended to party every night with my friends from school, swim in the pool, catch yabbies if there was water in the dam, and trash my brothers at tennis.

Newport must not have worked out because Genevieve brought me back a carved troll from a third world country she'd flown to during the hols. She looked buffed and even trimmer than usual. Probably cosmetic tourism. Since Hal had gone, no one had mentioned carbon footprints. I couldn't. Not when I was waiting for her approval to fly. Shower Butler was being launched at the National Water Conservation Conference in Hobart, Tassie.

I was sick of standing and watching water rush down the drain while I waited for it to get hot – ten per cent, apparently, totally wasted – so I did heaps of research on ways to recirculate water, then the engineers came on board, and Monica said saving four litres each shower was significant, as well as fantastic.

Production and packaging quotes kept arriving and the advertising text was ready to be signed off. Every Friday I had a catch-up with the promotions team before I reported what was ahead and behind schedule to Gen, plus projected costs. Every week she changed the colour scheme or the lettering font as well as giving me several impossible tasks. Like, 'You must have a product endorsement from Professor Phyllis Featherspoon at UCLA.'

Fuck. I hadn't seen a film or been to the theatre or cooked dinner for my Sydney friends in months. My best friend had stopped trying to contact me since I'd had to work late the day she had an abortion.

She'd texted: 'Obsession not just perfume name.'

Only swine flu and chemo made people feel this crook. I turned off the alarm, tossed off the blanket, pulled it back up again, and slept.

By nine that morning, when I finally got to work, Genevieve was sending my temp back to the agency for arriving half an hour late. The temp told her all trains from Hornsby had been delayed by a suicide on the tracks.

'Tell somebody who cares,' Genevieve yelled at the temp's back.

By lunchtime all my joints felt hammered. I made it to the toilet just in time. Twice. Gen was pacing outside the toilet door, waiting to thrust urgent media briefings at me. I wiped my hand across my mouth hoping I didn't smell too bad. I was too sick to write anything. I told her I'd phoned for a cab to go home and die.

'Cancel the cab. Don't leave until I've okayed them.'

An hour later, letters and numbers were playing chasings around each other in woozy circles so I e-mailed the briefings to her with apologies, downed more Aspros, grabbed a couple of plastic bags in case I vomited in the cab and sneaked down the rear stairs. The one time I really needed to take the lift, I didn't; running into her was too risky.

I returned with a doctor's certificate and apologies. Genevieve called me into her office. As a result of an audit, Accounts was being monitored.

'Not a word outside this office; jobs and reputations are at stake,' she said.

'I wouldn't gossip about Bili.'

'Fuck Biliyana. What about my reputation? I'm her supervisor. If the bitch offers to take on more work at the meeting, you offer as well, and I'll delegate everything to you.'

I couldn't handle any more work, and I wasn't an accountant for God's sake. But how could I say that? Genevieve and I air brushed and shredded everything.

'Take her name off the group e-mails.'

For months Bili had picked me up in her old Charade each morning and only let me buy petrol twice. She seemed more likely to take the worm farm home for the holidays than commit fraud, but it was career suicide to be seen with her outside. Genevieve said every grown up needed a car.

I still didn't have her signature. When I asked her, she sent me down to the food hall to buy her and Cody, the trainee, takeaways. He was too busy working on his job application to be a gopher.

'Must be something in those tiny champagne bubbles,' Monica said. 'She picked him up at Icebergs. Thinks he can manage a project because he's shaken a cocktail.'

Cody hung around my desk, curious about what I did, and raving about some drummer at the Coogee Bay Hotel on Fridays. He was four years younger than me but he really wanted me to hear this drummer.

'Sorry Sandee,' he said on Thursday. 'No can do the Coogee Bay mañana. Dinner and application writing marathon at Gen's.'

'She's running the panel, isn't she?'

'Yeah, my application has to be perfecto.'

'She's writing it *and* interviewing you?'

'So?' He tossed a shiny iPhone from one hand to the other. I could only guess she'd given it to him.

The rain came down just as the lift opened. I pressed the 'up' icon to go back to pick up my umbrella and raincoat. Cody was sitting on my chair, his boots on my desk, reading one of my files, drinking from my mug.

'Co-deee!'

'Chill, Goldilocks. Just getting up to speed for the interview.'

He was in the lift when I arrived Monday morning, dressed like he'd ridden a horse to work.

'Sorry about everything,' he said.

'The project's been nominated for a conservation design award at the conference. What's to be sorry about?'

'Flow with the go, babe.'

When I told Monica she said, 'Get your conference approval and flights signed off and update your CV. Someone at the conference is bound to be on the lookout for a reliable project manager.'

She whispered that she was forwarding an e-mail, from the Gen-eral. My name was no longer included in the group. The header was: Redistribution of project allocations.

I wanted to square my shoulders and march into Gen's office in my good suit, but it was at the cleaners. I regretted every training course I hadn't made time for. Every research article I hadn't finished. Every person upstairs I hadn't bothered sucking up to. I clenched the lapels of my jacket across my throat. I pictured a semi, loaded with water tanks, crushing a yellow Celica into a Harbour Bridge pylon, and knocked. I imagined all eyes on me.

'I need your signature to attend the conference in Hobart so I can book flights.' I was clutching my lip gloss, of all things, as though I wanted her to sign the wall with it.

'Sorry, Sandra. These decisions are made upstairs.'

'My conference paper has been accepted and the launch booked.'

'It's out of my hands.'

'The conservation design award will be announced at the dinner. If we win.'

'One of us can pick it up.'

She told me to give her my credit card. Not like, you're fired, just like don't use the credit card to fly to Hobart.

'Am I fired, then?'

She put her hand out for the card.

'No need to be dramatic,' she said, taking scissors from the desk drawer. Little wings of plastic fell into the recycling bin.

My bowels were churning even before she pointed her finger at my workstation where Cody was sitting. Roy from Security, was waiting. I could hear serious typing. Cody lifted the butterfly off my computer.

'You don't want this, do you?'

I nodded and caught it. Poor thing had done well to hang on for eight months. Next time I'd ask for a cockroach.

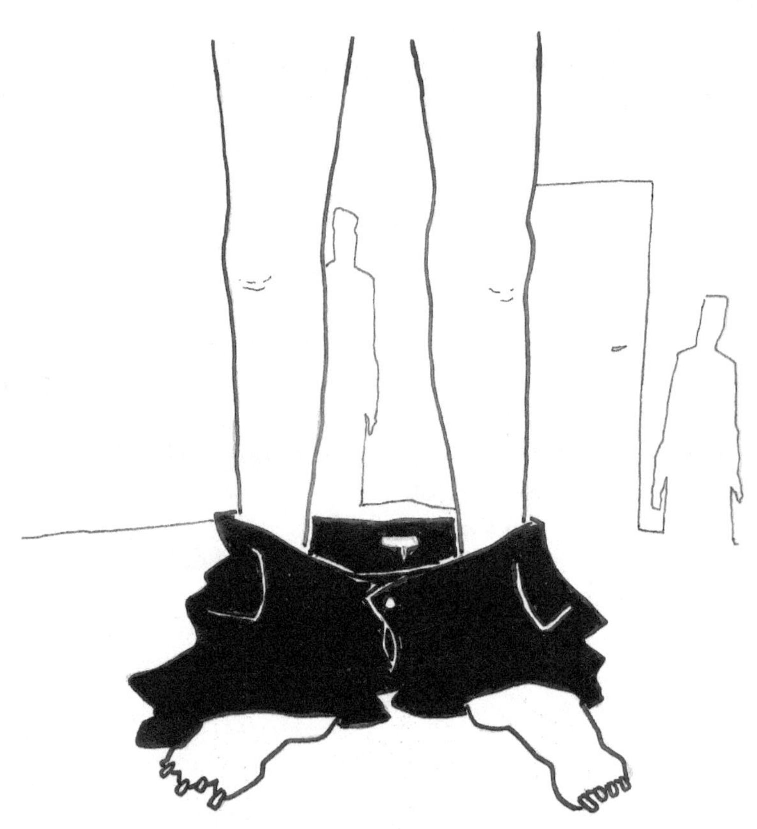

Kynon

Billy wasn't talking to me when he said, 'Ya Mum and Bro was stuffin' their gobs at Maccas in Dubbo.'

'Kynon's Mum's dead, you dick,' Jase said.

I stopped looking at the telly and looked at Jase, then Billy. My Mum was dead.

'Me cuz saw Cory and her eating at Maccas.'

'Whatever.' I shrugged it off. Concentrated on flicking a scab from a mozzie bite onto the brown plastic chair seat. Billy's cuz should know. While I was trying to cop it sweet, watching the telly in the Kariong common room, Cory'd been having an ace time with Mum. Shit! If this was true, and she wasn't dead, where'd she been all this time?

'Probably was Mrs Pincus, his foster mum.' I stood up and grabbed a spotty apple off the table. Last year's crop from some prison farm. The apples had been ponging like cider all week. Boys' homes sucked, even on the Central Coast.

'Zackly what I said on the phone. But me cuz said Cory called her *Mum* and she had brown hair and eyes like youse.'

Mrs Pink-arse'd had grey hair since dinosaurs roamed the Western Plains of New South Wales. I hadn't seen Cory since the coppers dumped me here, but if he'd been seeing Mum all along, he'd lied his arse off. I ate the whole apple including the tough shields that protected the seeds. Even the seeds themselves. Why hadn't Mum visited?

The next morning, Sunday, the wind howled through the trees and the frost was white on the grass when I pounded around the track. Wet brown leaves stinking of worms made the track slippery but nobody gave a fuck if I skidded and fell. Dunlop Volleys with soles worn smooth didn't help. My own foster mum farted on about brands made by Asian kids who should have been in school. She was always going sick about school and mums who drank and dads who bashed kids. After the Welfare had dumped Cory in Narromine and me in Dubbo I *had* to jig school to search all the school playgrounds until I found him. He was my responsibility.

I'd been awake half Saturday night having the old nightmare and my arms still ached. The water had come splashing over the tin roofs. I was trying to haul Mum from the flood, grabbing onto Cory tight so the water couldn't take him too. Heard her voice say, 'My boys, my beautiful boys' before she turned into a fish and swam away. Me and Cory hunched together on the roof. I yanked him in close. Same stupid dream. As though there were floods at Lightning Ridge. OK, that time everybody talks about decades ago but not while we lived there.

I slowed down my pace to let the S/Cape4 catch up. No sense trying to do a personal best when no one was holding a stop watch. Jase, Lou and Billy all wanted outa Kariong much as I did. We had this plan. During the screws' union meetings, when the dorm was quiet, we'd cut grey blankets into strips and plait them to make lug. Of course you could just steal a couple of extension cords and knot them every two metres but it's important to scale a wall honourably — on a moonless night just like the old safe crackers did. For a proper escape you needed a fog and a tall brick wall, preferably one with a tower and a sweeping floodlight. Lou and Jase were as eager as I was to use grappling hooks but the dorm was on the ground floor. The only brick wall was less than a metre high. It's stupid, having to find a wall every time you need to escape.

Jase had volunteered to eyeball for spots the floodlights missed. It was Lou's job to get hold of a phone and order pizzas. Ham and pineapple ones. Shame we wouldn't get to eat them. The delivery would be the signal. While the Super was looking through the boxes for his pizza supreme, I'd throw the grappling hooks attached to the lug. At the same time one of the Kooris had volunteered to threaten suicide, using the Abo flag as a noose. Bad taste but hell, his idea.

Billy had seen a show on telly about tunnelling out with a spoon and swallowing the dirt. It'd taken thirty-seven months, three weeks and five days. Get real. It'd been seven years since Mum had left.

'The delivery van'll take us straight to the pizza joint for fags,' Billy said.

He still didn't get the idea of the code among thieves. I tried to picture a man from a Most Wanted poster hitching a lift in a pizza van. Better to borrow a car.

There'd been no moonlight in the Ridge the night Mum left our shack on the Three Mile and of course none of the shacks had electric power. I'd woken in the dark, in bed with Cory, smelling chocolate. I heard a car door slam and saw the headlights ricochet around the walls. I was glad Cory stayed asleep so's I could hold him. She'd left a Tim Tam on each pillow. I ate mine, left his, although I wanted it. He could eat it for breakfast.

When I sneak into the dorm for the S/Cape4 meeting that arvo, Billy was already sitting on my bed wrapped in a blanket. Jase and Lou had visitors. Billy was older, but that hadn't stopped me decking him on the Narromine playground for dead-legging a kid. The same skanky rat-tail crawling down the back of his neck. He was mad keen to go 'cause he needed smokes; claimed he'd been smoking since he was three.

'Forget about tunnelling; forget about scaling walls. Us two are boltin' tonight,' he said.

Would Gramps have waited to do it the proper way? Probably. The old style crims were cool. But Billy and I were new style. Like addicts, we needed instant gratification. He stuck up his hand and I high-fived it. He needed fags bad.

At ten o'clock he pried open the dorm windows and

we climbed over the sills, dropped down, hit the ground and dashed across the field towards the highway. One wire fence. No problem. Last time I'd hot-wired a red Holden, while Billy checked out the sound system. No red Holdens. Only a tan root-ute. I was closest to the driver's seat. Bitch of a thing to start. A piece of shit but who cared?

A couple of hundred metres up the Pacific Highway he said, 'Shift, ya wuz!'

I didn't let on I'd never driven a manual.

'S'almos'outta juice.'

Every driver's door needs a gauge outside saying how much petrol's left so you don't waste time stealing one with an empty tank. I never heard of the old crims cracking an empty safe. 40 k's was shit slow and the stupid thing kept bucking. 'Hey, that sign says *Gosford.*'

'If we're goin' all the way ta Dubbo to find ya Mum and then goin' all the way back ta the Cross, we're gonna need petrol. Gotta cruise down to Gosford first. Jewellery shop… done it before.'

Duh. Would he disconnect the alarm this time? I dropped him out front, humped it around the back and stalled. He should be wearing gloves. The old blokes always wore gloves. At least we'd remembered to stuff our pillows under the blankets on the beds. I checked the glove box: chewing gum, maps and a warped snapshot. Picture of someone's mum. Unwrapped a stick of the dried out gum. Jiggled my legs. Flicked a few scabs. Drummed a beat on the wheel with my thumbs. Billy didn't know shit about alarm systems. Supposed to be out in less than ninety seconds; everybody knew that. The woman in the Polaroid looked pregnant, but it wasn't Mum. Mum's brown eyes had sparkles in them like opals. That old snap of her standing in front of the Bottle House at the Ridge after Dad'd cut her hair with his clippers; she didn't look all that old. I shouldn't have bothered emptying grog down the thunderbox; she always found more. And I shouldn't have ripped up that photo. Better to take a deep breath and count backwards from twenty.

The alarm blasted for two minutes and fifty-seven seconds before Billy ran out.

'I'm driving. Poofs like ya shouldn't be allowed ta drive.'

'I'm no poof.' I slammed the door and ran around to the passenger's seat before he drove off without me.

'Kings Cross, sluts and drugs, here we come! Where's the fuckin' lighter?' he yelled.

I turned up The Angels to drown him out. Why didn't he say he could shift? I was so busy watching for a sign to Dubbo I didn't realise we were back up the hill until I saw the petrol station with the buckets of flowers out front. Kariong, again. Something big had been going on. God, Billy was stupid, doubling back like that. He drove straight through, fast. At Mt Kuring-gai there were sirens, lights and a blockade of cop cars – an ambush at gun point just like on telly.

'What took you so long?' said a cop, shining his torch in.

'What're ya bragging about? Ya didn't pull off a break and enter.'

God, Billy was a dick. They snapped on handcuffs and ordered us into the paddy wagon.

'Hey, no seat belts,' I told them. The way they threw you around on those hard benches, that was dangerous. 'You crash and we'll sue.'

At the holding cells the coppers strip-searched me and took the chewing gum right out of my mouth. Like, where were you supposed to get more chewie? Maybe they thought it was drugs or pills or shit. I shouldn't have ripped up her photo. But they'd have taken it. Scum who'd steal chewie right outa your mouth.

They removed the hand cuffs, gave us a meat pie each and coffee, yuck, and locked us in cells with real crims.

'Jist lads,' a stupid cop said.

Mum not giving a rat's was heaps worse than her being dead.

Kynon has his photo taken

'Thanks, but I need more than a cuppa to be able to write you a classo report, Kynon.'

'I need a good report to be moved to medium security, that's what you said, Chalkie.'

'This is an *Education* Office. You've only submitted one unit, one mediocre unit.'

With three hundred and forty prisoners going before the Classification Committee every six months Cathie spent a lot of time sitting at the desk typing reports. Nothing surprised her anymore. When she first took the job as Education Officer her friends phoned to hear her stories. Now they advised her to get another job.

Today Kynon in his green uniform sits opposite her. 'I don't want to rot here for another six months. Can't I owe you or something?'

'Thought about doing Reading and Writing for Adults?'

'Bor-ing.'

'Definitely more boring than Coastal Navigation.'

'You want to lecture me, Chalkie? Or hear why I can't study?'

'Landing drugs on remote beaches by moonlight will get you back in here faster than a speeding bullet. It's a wank.'

'You have something against wanking?'

'Get a grip, Kynon.'

'I should spend more time with Mrs Palm and her five daughters?'

'All right.' Cathie sighs, and turns away from the computer screen. 'Tell me why you can't study, and it'd better be good this time.'

'Last night this thug was thrown in my cell.' He checked she was paying attention.

'You're the only one two-out with a crim? Pull the other one.'

'The screw said, "Here's trouble." '

'Who did you expect – somebody's grandpa in for re-gluing unfranked postage stamps?'

'This was a career man. Huge pecs. Tatts. Bruised veins. LICK on one fist. BASH on the other. I thought he was gonna rape me.'

'You don't expect me to write that in a report?'

'I woke up with him shaking me.'

Cathie leans forward.

Kynon whispered, 'It was Rispoli. I was shit scared. He started going through my stuff.'

'Drugs?'

'Said, "Mate, mate, any chilli, mate?" '

'Chilli?' She looks puzzled.

'That's what I thought. Said he wanted black pepper and when I didn't have any, he threw my instant coffee all over.'

'That is a new one.'

'Puts the sniffer dogs off.'

'You want some of my instant – '

'Only if you can spare some. Rispoli was stuffing things everywhere and I swallowed the stash of sugar I was saving to make a brew.'

'I suppose you want more?' Cathie sighed.

He looked at her, 'Only if you can spare some, Chalkie.'

She looked at her robust wrist, a man's watch. 'The siren's about to go.'

'At 3 a.m. these four blokes from the Emergency Unit charge in with batons, shields and a video camera. More were stomping around the corridor. They're yelling, "Strip. Over there. Fast. Move it. Faster, both a' youse." I let my clothes drop, what could I do? And one yelled "Take off the socks, Rispoli. Youse know the rules." '

'You gotta hurry. Tell me later.' Cathie looks out the window at the men in green lining up for muster.

'Legs spread, facing the wall, my hands on the cold sandstone. I heard the click and whirr of the video. "Squat and spread your cheeks. Turn this way. Stick out your tongue, pull out your cheeks. No, the other cheeks, arseholes!" '

'Go. You'll be late.'

Kynon stands up, leans forward, both hands spread on the desk. 'One shines a torch in my mouth. Sniffer dogs drag my bedding onto the floor. Finally, the video camera clicks off. The Alsatians and all but two of the men leave. I think we're off scot-free until I hear the video camera click on again.'

'Run.'

'Tell you the rest this arvo.'

Locked up in the wing after lunch Kynon writes his story. He'd been at Mt Penang the weekend they ran a video workshop.

Reading and Writing for Adults!!!

Title: **MR CLIPBOARD PLANTS THE HASH!!!**
by Kynon Walter Reiff

Thursday. Night. Inside wing.
Kynon and Rispoli's cell. 3.11 a.m.

Scene one: A hand in a transparent glove drops a chunk of hash on a shelf.

Scene two: Mr Clipboard, an Emergency Unit officer, lifts his hand in a transparent glove and takes off his helmet. Close up: his dial happy as, when he discovers the hash right there on the shelf.

Scene three: He confiscates it.

Scene four: A gloved hand scrawls on the clipboard. 'R. Rispoli. Possession. One chunk hash.'

Scene five: Rispoli is dragged off to the slammer screaming.

MONDAY. MORNING MUSTER. OUTDOORS.
YARD IN MIDDLE OF WINGS. 8.45 A.M.

Scene six: CLOSE UP: groovy boobs (only kidding!!!).
CLOSE UP: young screwess winks as she unlocks the gate. 'You're a porn star, Kynon.'
'Star idiot, you mean.'
'A freckle big as a five cent piece on your left bun!'
'Huh?'
'The Emergency Unit videos at the barbie yesterday. You'd a pissed yourself!'

THE END

Kynon extends his hand which is holding the story towards Cathie, 'Trade you, for a classo report.'

Videos you can jerk off to

Kynon was more like a safe cracker than a junkie. In for spraying graffiti, escaping from boys' homes, joy-riding and hot wiring. A nineteen-year-old nuisance to society rather than a real crim. After the lunchtime muster, he'd passed Wanda leaving Chalkie's education office.

Anywhere I wanda, anywhere I room, till I'm in the arms of my psy-chol-o-gist, my heart won't have no home.

That tune had been stuck in his groove for days. Obsession or just boredom? He was clueless. When he watched Thommo and the other crims walking through the yard staring at her tits, her legs, her arse, he wanted to punch their lights out. When he was locked up in his cell at night, while the porn was broadcast, he tried to remember every detail about her that differed from the day before. He remembered the stockings she wore, whether she had a different watch. He tried to work out why her copper-coloured hair, where it jutted down towards her right eyebrow, had ridges some mornings and not others. After a fortnight of observation and jerking off, he decided it had to be sex. If Wanda was fucking some prick, she washed her hair before they went to bed at night. But if she wasn't getting any, she showered in the morning.

He made himself sick worrying about her infidelity to him but even if she was fucking a grease with black curls and an earring, he was powerless. What she did outside had to be her own business. For now, anyway. All he needed was a few excellent Classification Reports to get Early Release and be on the bus to Bondi Junction before Thommo was out. Kynon pictured how pleased Wanda would be when she opened the door at 5/114 Capri Parade, and saw him standing in the hall in his own jeans and red hoodie. He reckoned she'd be untying the laces of a see-through chocolate nightie as she headed for the shower. She'd let him stay, maybe for just one night at a time, until she got to know him and he could move in.

Waiting to be called for his appointment with her, Kynon noticed the dark shapes of the damp seeping through the sandstone walls of the corridor. The officer in charge of industries had this nineteenth-century sandstone wall, this wall chiselled with initials and cryptic marks, on his list: two coats of impermeable membrane tinted different colours and painted in opposite directions so you could see that everything was covered properly, followed by a couple of coats of thick gloss. Along with the other students in the TAFE painting and decorating course, Kynon was expected to obliterate history with pink paint. Desecration. When he talked about heritage nothing happened. No one was interested in how jails used to look.

He appreciated the texture of the sandstone while he waited to see Wanda. Better to wait than be embarrassed by hearing his name and MIN number called over a loudspeaker. He knew the risks of ending up in D Ward as well as any other inmate. No one was going to mess with his mind but he was willing to risk one appointment, just to be alone with her. And the excellent report she would write for the Classification Committee would oil his progression through the system. Maximum. Medium. Minimum. Out the gate.

Thommo was her inmate clerk. If he wasn't snuffling around inside her office, he was hanging around the corridor, watching for crims to leave.

He stopped in front of Kynon and darted his hand out of his pocket, pointed to the office door. 'Pongs like brothel pong, don't it?'

If Kynon nodded yes, Thommo would demand to know everything he knew about hookers, but if Kynon hesitated, Thommo would accuse him of being a poof.

Thommo stretched a few strands of his hair across his mouth and sucked them in.

Wanda opened the door.

'Prostitutes again, Thommo? Interesting,' she said.

Thommo didn't get regular appointments to see her. Lifers were required to get reports for the Serious Offenders Board from a real shrink.

She turned. New glasses with green frames. 'With *you* in a sec, Kynon.'

She knew his name and pronounced it slowly, caressing it with her lips until it sounded splendid. Three hundred and forty green tee-shirts and green track suit pants weren't enough green? Green glasses? She would never wear anything green when he got out.

Except on visits, crims didn't get to see many women. Besides Wanda and Chalkie, there was the welfare officer, a few teachers, a handful of custodial officers and one trannie. Most were lezzos; even so, they owed it to the crims to wear bright colours to cheer the place up.

Last week in Budget Cooking they'd had an eighty-year-old nun teaching them how to make festive salad with boiled lentils, tinned pineapple and beetroot. Kynon and Thommo had to wash up. As soon as Thommo's long white arms matted with black hairs were immersed in suds, he claimed he'd been watching screwesses and visitors for twelve years and had also been lucky enough to observe women in hospital, once and court, twice. Then he boiled over like fermented brew. Breasts! Bosoms! Bust! Boobs! Titties! Tits! Knockers! Jugs!

The saucepan lid slipped out of Kynon's hands and clattered to the floor. By the time he stood up again, Thommo was describing Wanda's lacy black stockings with the arrows shooting up the backs of her legs. The washing up water was frothy with activity. He raved on about sheer stockings and cursed thick ribbed ones; her stockings, apparently, were codes just for him.

Kynon didn't say anything, just reached across into the pink scum to pull the plug before the sink overflowed.

'Black garters pressed into white fe-lesh.'

Thommo's spit sprayed the clean dishes. With clenched fists he wrung the water from each tea towel. Kynon was relieved Thommo lusted after Wanda, not him.

Thommo claimed to protect her by meeting the crims in the corridor before and after they'd been in to see her. He advised them how to keep their secrets safe from her in exchange for her personal information. He knew her post box number, phone number and address, real estate agent; he knew the licence number of her old green Datsun; he knew the names of the Thai veggo curries she ordered at her favourite restaurant on Campbell Parade in Bondi. He knew Opium was her favourite perfume; he knew the names of her sister's daughters, their address and school.

He advised Kynon, 'Invent a problem or she'll claw her way in your head and you'll hear about your issues at every class-o.'

Saliva sprayed each time Thommo said *issues*. Kynon hoped it didn't carry HIV. He needed a problem he could overcome easily, one that would guarantee good reports. The topics Oprah and Dr Phil featured seemed way too complicated.

Now Wanda waved Thommo away calling, 'There's some filing you can do later.' She pointed to the chair by her desk and told Kynon she'd be with him as soon as she finished her notes.

Kynon glanced around, searching for something to tell Thommo. Twisted ivy almost strangled her teapot and the pink scarf tied over a lampshade made a rosy glow on the walls and ceiling. Something about the light reminded him of the kero lamps at the shack on the Three Mile at Lightning Ridge where he'd grown up – corrugated tin, cement floor, grey fibro, plastic ribbons hanging in the doorway, cartons stacked with empties. Father picked up a second-hand generator to keep his beer cold the week before he called the welfare to come and get the boys. Kynon never tasted ice cream until he lived in a foster home. Wanda's rosy light was too much. He was already thinking about childhood shit.

In her office a safe was hidden under a sarong. Kynon could see a bulge in the silk made by the combination lock. Even if someone broke into the office the stories people told her would be safe. Safe in a safe. He chuckled. She swivelled around.

Before she sneaked in an embarrassing question, before she tried to manipulate his mind, he reeled off the goals Chalkie had made him write out in the Education Office, 'I need to work on improving communication and relationship skills and developing job skills.'

Wanda pressed her biro to her lips. 'I'm hearing you say you'd prefer to talk to a vocational counsellor or a parole officer. Is that right, Kynon?'

'I need to talk to a real psychologist, such as yourself, one who understands crims.'

Her lips broke into a grin. He'd said the right thing. He knew from the communications group that avoiding eye contact made you look shifty. But what good did knowing that do?

Her glasses were such a foul green his eyes kept veering over to the spines of the books on her shelf. *Abnormal Psychology*. *Deviant Behaviour*. Warped shit for his lady to be reading. He imagined her taking notes from the piles of books on her bedside table, under a lamp with a crimson scarf slung over the shade. She tucked the sheet up under her arms, covering her sweet tits. She wouldn't read in bed if he was there.

'If you want to work with me, we need to start with your earliest memories, mm?'

He helped himself to a tissue from the box on the desk, twisted it, untwisted it, smoothed it, smelled it, then blew his nose to get some time. Well they weren't about sex, that was for sure.

'The first thing you remember?'

'Father's dog sprawling over me, trying to bite my stomach. The sweaty smell when Father came home from mining opal.'

'Your *first* memories. Do you remember being breastfed?'

'God, no! Sorry. Am I supposed to?'

He should have prepared his answers with Thommo.

'Mum…' He paused. What could he say to show how much care he'd taken of his mum?

'I'm not your Mum, Kynon, however suitable re-parenting might be.'

She looked pleased and smoothed upwards the stocking on one leg, then the other. 'If you could wave a magic wand and change one thing about your childhood what would it be?'

He needed something weirder than a mum who drank. But if he said something too weird, she might transfer him to the shrink who locked everybody away in D ward. He pushed on the hard-on tucked into the elastic waist of his shorts.

'Just one thing?'

'One thing.'

'Only one thing?'

'So what's distracting you, Kynon?'

He was relieved when a toilet flushed somewhere behind the wall.

'We'd have a flush toilet, indoors, instead of the thunderbox. That's what I'd change.'

The dunny'd been built of dead marines over an abandoned mine shaft, lit only by stars, on the nights there were stars. He couldn't remember the number of times an old roo had pivoted on the track back to the shack, frightening him but mostly he'd been afraid of falling, falling down into the long mine shaft.

As she leaned back, the edge of her silver ballet shoe brushed against his leg. She frowned. 'You want to use this time we have together to tell me about *an outhouse*?'

It was too soon to tell her what he was thinking. Her notes looked, from his upside down perspective like, *avoidance of … mothering issues*. Was she accusing him of not having looked after his Mum well enough? Her writing was pretty loopy. *Anal fix … Fuck!* he thought, *Kinky.* No one was going to mess with *his* bum.

'Let's move along to masculinity and the fathering relationship.'

He wondered if the second button on her satiny-smooth blouse had just slipped. Her bra, where the sun tan stopped, was glossy as chocolate icing. He wet his lips. Women liked it when you said their name during sex.

'In what ways do you plan to be like your dad, Kynon?'

Fuck. Best not mention guns. 'Like my dad?'

'Kynon, try to stay with me.'

He was tangled up, shifting around and she was twisting around too. Or maybe she was mirroring his body language to make him feel comfortable. The group had had a session on that.

'Lots of attractive, intelligent young men model themselves on their dads.'

'Not on mine.'

'OK, tell me about that.' She glanced at her wrist.

In solitary Kynon hadn't been able to stop thinking about him. 'The sun won't shine out of any dog's ass. I'd treat my woman like a goddess. I wouldn't drink myself stupid and bash people. If anyone came to take *my* kids, I'd run 'em off with a shotgun.'

He realised he'd said too much. 'Can I go now?'

'As soon as you've told me two things you respect him for.'

'Respect?' He bit the skin at the edge of his thumbnail.

Her hand, stroking her throat and chest, made her tits jiggle up and down, one after the other. He leaned so far forward he could smell the perfume rising from between them.

'He drew faces on his biceps so I could watch them move up and down; he yanked off beer caps with his teeth.'

'You're doing so well, Kynon.' Her eyelashes bounced double time behind the lenses.

'When do I get to see you again?'

'Now Kynon, what do you want to get from our sessions?'

He looked at the floor. 'Use my time to advantage.' Thommo would be waiting in the corridor. The personal stuff he was supposed to find out. His head raced. Favourite team? Show? Food? Song? Position? Magazine? Not a lezzo are you?

'I like the glasses. Where'd you get 'em?' he asked.

'These lenses aren't prescription ones, just pretend, to make me present as more serious to the officers on the Classo Committee this arvo. Look.'

She handed them to him. Thin red lines edged the green plastic. They smelled like shampoo. He peered through them and handed them back.

'Can I borrow a book till next time?' he pointed toward the bookcase.

'This isn't a lending library. Books are like hearts. Give your heart freely but never lend it, Kynon.'

'I have an awful lot of problems, Wanda. I need to see you more than once a week.'

The swishing noise was Wanda uncrossing her legs.

Fishing

Cathie waited outside. It was 9.38 a.m. before the heavy door swung open and a custodial officer stepped aside.

'Thanks. Humid, isn't it?' Cathie ducked as she stepped over the metal bar, into the jail. She felt as though the climate should be different inside, but it was just as hot. December weather everywhere. The officer stared straight ahead with his lips pressed together. Cathie stepped in front of him and turned right.

Today was the day of the Christmas lunch, the last day before the long holiday break. She lifted bags bulging with food onto the counter for inspection and swung her backpack up next to them. She signed in, last, at 9.42. Usually she was the first of the professional staff to arrive. Usually her bags bulged with education supplies. The officer behind the window managed a quick smile.

'Big day, eh, Chalkie?' He waved her through. Probably he was anxious to get back to his toast. Jails always smelled of burnt toast.

'Thanks. Have a good one.'

She took a deep breath of the sandalwood essence she wore like a protective cape, and braced her shoulders to walk through three hundred and forty men milling around in the circular yard. Wedge-shaped sandstone buildings, the wings where the cells were, radiated from the circle.

Although she walked through this bitumen yard several times every working day it was always the first time, always challenging her image of who she was. She wanted to give inmates opportunities to better themselves. She wanted them to have the skills to hold down jobs when they got out. Riggers, dogmen and fork lift drivers who were clean and didn't need to sell drugs to survive. Even vacuuming pubs was better than dealing.

As the third gate clanked she visualised a path parting the sea of green uniforms and tugged her cream linen jacket tighter across her chest. A woman could never be covered in enough layers in a jail. The men who'd come in overnight looked seedy in comparison to the tanned muscular regulars. The ones who didn't know her gawked but she could cope with that. She was swerving to dodge a ball when she caught sight of Stan, in his blue uniform, shuffling toward the gate to the Education Area, the key in his hand, ready to unlock it for her and the crims falling into line behind her. One of the bricklaying students waved.

'The radio says it'll hit thirty-six degrees,' she called out to Stan.

'Just gotta tell ya, Chalkie, Maisie's phoned in sick.'

Not today. Of all days. 'Thanks for telling me Stan.'

She felt enormous crossing the goldfish pond on the stepping stones behind him. Sucking up to officers made her feel like spewing. He fiddled with his keys and unlocked one more gate and she walked through and unlocked the office door herself. 10.03 a.m. Straight into the stench of stale smoke.

She cranked the window open. Looked out at the brick walls. Rested her eyes on the pond. Some of the regulars, the career men, waited to roll cigarettes until they left the education office but the new young blokes showed no respect. Only yesterday one had said, *'Smokin's me only pleasure, Miss, unless you want to sit on me nose.'* She had just managed to stop herself from saying, *Your nose is longer than your dick?*

Maisie was supposed to pick up the pavlovas this morning before she cruised the jail spruiking to get bums on seats in the classes.

Roll up! Roll up! If computers aren't your thing, literacy, numeracy, lunacy, or an art class perhaps?

Cathie did the education admin while Maisie saw that the classes ran smoothly. Inmates on their way to the computer room or library stuck their heads through the office door on the lookout for Maisie. Cathie greeted most by name. One stopped to tell her he'd had a Christmas card from his daughter and pulled a photo out of his pocket. The same old wrinkled photo. Another asked her to write a love poem for his girlfriend in another jail. Cathie added his name to the list for the literacy class. Students enrolled in correspondence courses checked to see if their units of study had been marked and returned although the mail didn't arrive until afternoon. The inmate computing clerk rushed in to start booting up computers as soon as he saw the teacher crossing the circle. The main classroom where the lunch would be was to the left of the office. Gav, the inmate clerk, was already there, spreading butchers' paper and plastic cutlery on tables.

Prisoners were not allowed to get their hands on anything they could ferment but Cathie had succumbed to their pressure and requested permission to bring in fruit. The Superintendent had said if she'd go out for a drink with him, he'd trust her to use her discretion about what she brought in, so, what the hell, one kilo of cherries and a wedge of watermelon. She stashed them behind everything else in the fridge. Some of the lifers wouldn't have tasted cherries in a decade. Some crims would never have tasted one.

Sitting at the desk she could feel the sweat trickling down behind her knees. She had asked Stan to enforce a rule: the men had to wear jocks under their green nylon shorts to be allowed into the education area. Dangling testicles were too much. Maisie agreed.

'Oops a daisy,' Maisie had said – was it yesterday? – as she deliberately let a pair of metal scissors and a metal ruler fall, clanking and clattering together long enough for erections to subside.

Cathie'd have to go out and pick up the pavlovas herself.

One of the crims, Terry, burst through the gate – yellow plastic boots and a yellow raincoat – waving a long stick. Terry often clowned around, but how could he stand wearing plastic in this heat?

Gav leaned against the office doorway, weight on one leg, jiggling the other. Terry stood outside the office window, aggressively knotting safety pins and paper clips onto string. Undoubtedly nicked from her desk. Should she hang around to find out what he was up to? Gav watched without commenting. Gav's people had been real fishermen; generations of them had fished off the coast. From the art room he could stare at the Tasman Sea through the window. His people still lived at La Perouse; LaPa, he called it.

She slid the window shut so Terry wouldn't be tempted to reach in for the phone. The pavlovas. She should go but she wanted to spend as much time with Gav as she could. Would he miss her during the hols? Of course he would. Although perhaps he'd miss gorgeous Maisie even more.

'Pity about Maise. Want help with the food or anything?' Gav asked.

'About Maisie?' This man was offering to help her. No one ever offered to help her.

'Breaking her hugging arm and all.'

The crims' voices outside overpowered the ghetto blaster. She could use a crowd wrangler. Terry, going through the motions of fishing, had snagged his line in the sapling with seven leaves. Why did men have to be so fucking loud?

'Broke her *hugging* arm?'

'Oops a daisy,' Gav shouted back, giving a wink.

'Oops a daisy, yourself. How'd she break it?'

He shrugged sheepishly.

'I'm going out to pick up the pavlovas.' Later she'd have to deal with how he was getting messages he shouldn't be. She wished Maisie was still going out with that drummer.

She couldn't leave until Stan returned with the keys.

By ten-forty-five, rapists, junkies and axe murderers she barely recognised were trashing the fishpond and the garden, if you were inclined to call a sapling, a few weeds and an assortment of twigs a garden and she was locked in with them. She sighed.

'Don't worry about them,' Gav said. He drew his finger along her hand and wrist as he lowered himself astride the chair reversed on the other side of the desk. 'Nothing to do with you.'

She reached into a shopping bag, pulled out a cylinder of Pringles, fanned some on a plate and passed it to Gav. Week after week the clerks had worked for pocket money. Six students were getting TAFE certificates and another one had come fifth in the state in bricklaying. Her stars. This celebration had to be perfect.

After she and Gav had finished three-quarters of the Pringles, she broke the heel off one of the bread sticks and gnawed on it. She'd put on so much weight she felt like she was wearing a down-filled jacket.

Where was Stan anyway? She had to get the pavs. 'I've got to get out of here.'

'Me too.' He picked up one crisp at a time. 'You need a gentleman to help carry the boxes?'

She gave him a look. Why did he have to be a crim? Sometimes she imagined spending whole days without running out of things to talk about. If only she could take him home.

'Just offering.'

Mud thudded against the window. She jumped. Terry, still in yellow, was stomping through the pond. His mates in green were too busy chucking water at each other to notice her schoolmarm scowl.

Gav leaned across the desk and lowered his voice. His bare leg brushed against hers. He glanced toward the window and back.

'Don't worry about the pav. In ten years no one will remember.'

'I want it to be special.'

'I swear on a stack of watermelon. It'll be special. Trust me.'

Trust him? Not on her sweet Nellie. It had been a long time since she'd trusted a man and Long Bay wasn't the place to start.

She wondered if the Super was aware of the disturbance. She should probably phone him but she didn't want Gav to think she was a dobber. And if she did phone, the Super would say she owed him another drink to celebrate the holidays. She followed Gav into a classroom, admired the way he'd arranged it, returned to the office alone, shut the door and picked up the phone.

'Education, Sir,' she said. The Super had high cholesterol and carried too much weight. Maybe there were Long Bay genes for it. At least her hair was still brown and wasn't receding. During a coffee break at an orientation session he'd told her that every week he dealt with a prisoner seducing one of his officers. Usually a female officer was caught giving head jobs in one of the towers. He didn't get it. In the old days officers'd bashed the crims senseless at every opportunity. He didn't approve of that either.

'Call you back,' he said.

The Super had never been terse before.

Well, she'd tried to warn him something funny was going on. It was a shame she couldn't send Gav out to pick up the pavs. Stan was standing at the gate again. Cathie unlocked the drawer, took out her wallet and locked the office.

'What's going on?' he asked.

She shrugged and handed him the list of who'd be coming back for lunch after muster. With the prisoners watching, she felt like she was colluding with the enemy. She looked at her watch. She wouldn't get back in time.

She returned to the office, unlocked it and helped Gav carry the bags of groceries to the classroom. Outside he'd done despicable things but she had to trust someone, and it was only food. He'd told her about his nightmares. She'd never met a more sensitive, thoughtful man. She honestly hadn't.

She was putting out the bread rolls when the sirens started. Had she done something to activate them? No. Grandiosity. She moved closer to the phone.

Inmates were lining up in the circle. Just muster. She checked her watch. Too early. The radio was blaring and Terry's mates outside the window were making whooping noises and squelching around imitating animals. Some officers arrived to usher them out the gate, into the circle, into lines. More sirens started. No wonder the Super hadn't flirted.

Gav came to the office door, rolled his eyes big-time, as if to say *told you*, and winked, before he pulled on his serious face. 'Thanks, Chalkie. Really. Thanks heaps. Oh, good hols and all …'

Thanks heaps? Good hols? He'd be back in ten minutes. His shiny green shorts bulged. Where was Maisie when she needed her? Then again his shorts would have bulged more frequently if Maisie were there.

Cathie remembered she still hadn't asked how he knew about the broken arm. Rats. Maisie must have given him her phone number. She'd have to deal with them later, both of them.

'See you after muster,' she called, but he'd gone. She went outside and snapped off the ghetto blaster. God, it was hot. She could hear counting over the loud speaker. Names called out, recounted, then all the crims were herded into the wings for lock-up. The sirens continued even after the circle was empty.

Teams of officers arrived and began searching the pond and garden area, her office, the store room, the computer room, the library and the big classroom. One picked up a bread roll and began munching. Whatever they were searching for – drugs or weapons, she supposed – wasn't in the toilet either.

Why the fuck didn't someone tell her what was going on?

Why didn't the Super keep her informed? All this talk about officers and professionals working together. Ha! She put the barbecued chooks back in the fridge before an officer nicked them. She overheard one of the officers say, *escapee* and stole a glimpse at his clipboard. *Laundry worker, MIN #* something she couldn't read. *Missing at muster.* The officer saw her looking and covered the clipboard before she saw the DOB. She never memorised their MIN numbers. One of the crims who worked in the laundry must have gone over the wall. Lucky it wasn't one of the education clerks or students. Or Gav.

The sirens stopped. She could see officers escorting the teachers across the circle toward the main gate which was ajar. Silence.

The legs of the chair at the head of the table scraped as she pulled it out. 'In ten years no one will remember Santa didn't stop at Long Bay,' she whispered hoarsely to herself. Her friends would say she sounded overwrought, but she was determined to remember the lunch without the guests of honour even if no one else did. *I swear on a stack of watermelon … it'll be special … trust me.*

She piled her plate with potato salad, used a plastic fork and her fingers to pull the breast meat from one of the chickens. When she was finished eating she licked off the grease, then washed her hands before she addressed and decorated big envelopes, even remembered to draw palm trees and beach umbrellas for the Muslims, then dropped in the chocolates, course certificates and greeting cards. She knew there'd be no chance to distribute the envelopes or even say *Happy Christmas* until February. Might as well eat the cherries.

The fridge was empty. No cherries. *Thanks, Chalkie. Really. Thanks heaps.* Gav, that con man. She hoped he wouldn't get caught with a brew.

She tipped the chocolates out of the envelopes and one by one unwrapped the red foil. They'd have been stale by February.

Cathie squinted back over her shoulder in the late afternoon glare as she walked toward the parking lot. She imagined she'd told Gav to call her Cathie and given him her phone number. He could be moved to another jail before the holiday ended. What would she do for the next six weeks? In the winter it had been dark when she gave her farewell glance to the sandstone walls and towers. Now, the sun, although low, was still hot. All the clerks and students were safely locked in their cells for the night and not out scamming and in danger. Her mobile rang. Maisie.

'God, I missed you today,' Cathie said. 'What did you do to your hugging arm?'

'My *arm*? Absolutely nothing, why?'

'Oh shit.' Bloody Gav.

'The dog had a run in with a Ducati,' Maisie said. 'I knew you wouldn't have your mobile so I asked the Super to pass on the message.' She groaned. 'Now I owe him another drink. That's six at least.'

'Your dog okay?' They could have a drink with the Super together. Hell, he'd have forgotten by February.

'The dog's leg is broken. Don't suppose you were able to put on the lunch?'

'How'd you know?'

'I heard on the car radio that a prisoner'd escaped in a laundry van while inmates distracted the officers by fishing. Our pond, I thought. God, Cath, tell me it wasn't Gav.'

Cathie's day

a quick squizz to the left on the drive to work
    sun blinks on sea
    the Datsun in front slams on its brakes
       don't drive faster than your Guardian Angel can fly
        Cathie and her G A fly in formation
        nineteen k an hour up Anzac Parade
          making them too fucking late to get a
          good parking spot

in the education area a new lean prisoner squints
    bloody eye socket   lip
    he clutches broken glasses, a tooth   spits.
    hiv splashes grey lino
       where's the art class
       hide me he begs
  she pivots him around by the elbow spins him out
  the door down the steps
       red-crosses the circle past three hundred forty
       metaphorical iron bars and real jeers
         paedophilehomoqueerpoofter
         rockierockierockie
         missscumbitchcunt who does she think she is
           defending the guilty
blood splashes her mosquito bite-scratched legs
she leads him through gates to a custodial officer
    iron-barred
    get him out of here
    they'll kill him

she doesn't know this crim she's rescuing.

when he is safely on the other side she quakes back across the circle
        tasting haematite
        a fist of fear lodged in her stomach,
        rushes for the toilet she shares with rapists and murderers
                since she's talked to the union
                a lock's been installed
                on the door a six year old could kick flat

her favourite crim tells her:
        show emotion Chalkie
        burst into tears
        they need to see you're angry
after lunch
Cathie's summoned to the super's office
        for telling officers how to do their job.
                her Guardian Angel's picnicking
                on some headstone
                at Waverley

at her flat Cathie paces
        around high carbs
        honey toast cocoa chocolate booze

her father at the carver end of the table
took the slices of beef
left crusts and dripping

                                he owned anger

when she was two
        she picked the heads off the neighbours' marigolds
        wiped her hands on their drying sheets
                who was looking after me
                when she'd fallen down a curb a third her height

                                    PERMISSION TO LIE

and rolled under a parked car she'd been smacked
where was my angel
has scars
not even the memory of anger
that night at the counselling course: another scenario:
a retired husband cast a fly into a lake
frightened the bird his wife had just focused on
each time he cast   another splash   more wings
what should his wife have said

big fucking whoop
the syllabus has no space for
iron bars
syringes of contaminated blood
paedophiles
toilets shared with rapists

during the break Cathie queues
for pumpkin soup
the most useful thing the course can provide
her G A's wings rustle, don't forget me
Cathie grabs two bowls
remembering that squizz at the sea

This awful brew

If the sun were out you might have veered off to Maroubra Beach and forgotten all about visiting Gav Cooke, justifying your existence and the whole jail catastrophe, but it is raining. You drive on.

A custodial officer in blue appears and the jail gate opens and just as promptly shuts, excluding you and the other visitors clustered under umbrellas. Someone inside the sandstone walls must be watching a monitor. It's already 10 a.m. and you're anxious to prove your work has been worthwhile, that at least one prisoner is continuing to study and isn't using. Hard to believe that until a few months ago you'd been in charge of the education of these prisoners. Besides being the most enthusiastic student, Gav Cooke had been your inmate clerk.

Your hand itches to push the buzzer until a man lifts a small girl who relieves you of all responsibility by pressing it. You're paranoid, imagining the surveillance camera swivels. Following you because you worked here? Possibly. One visitor is yelling and waving her bare arms in a jerky backstroke. You're the only one wearing a raincoat. You like to have as much of your body covered as possible.

A car skids and stops. Doors open and young Asians, one with blond streaks, race to the gate. Rain spots their white shirts. Rain drips off the brim of a Koori father's Akubra, drips on the bare shoulders of a redhead who's rolling up the waistband of her skirt. Her legs must ache from standing in those boots.

The gate swings open and the officer orders a man to take the child down from his shoulders. He orders the redhead to pick up her baby and collapse her stroller, ready for searching.

You stand at the sign-in desk holding your ID. The later

you arrive, the less time you'll get to stay. The stooped man ahead laboriously prints numbers on a card. A bald officer passes the stooped man's licence to a hirsute colleague. The officers pass the licence back and forth, marvelling at how one way the writing is the right way up and the other way the photo is. They wave the man through, then run their fingers down creased computer printouts, down the food-spotted computer screen itself, before agreeing that Cooke, #899472, the inmate you have come to visit, has been sent to Goulburn. Bugger, bugger, bugger.

'When?'

'Dunno. I saw a crim looked like him going out to run laps,' says the hairy officer.

You look at your watch. The bald one rechecks Gav's number and phones the wing.

'He's there, hanging around,' they chortle, handing you a see-through satchel for your belongings.

Muttering families crowd the entryway behind you. The bald officer upends a stroller and shakes it until a baby bottle filled with orange cordial bounces on the cobblestones. You follow the arrows pointing to the Visitor's Waiting Room, turn around in time to see the redhead pick up the bottle, wipe the nipple on her hip and thrust it at the baby.

One of the officers must say something you don't hear because the redhead screams, 'Search a baby? Piss orf, you sick old pervert. You got somethin' about baby bums or what?'

'Officers found contraband in his nappy at Parramatta.'

'The filth planted that! I'll tell my guy, youse are all perverts!'

To the right of the corridor a toilet door is ajar. The overhead cistern drips and rust oozes through the pipes. You imagine a sign, *Last place to shoot up before visiting.*

In the waiting room you join gaunt tattooed westies jiggling and scratching in front of a wall-mounted telly. Kids whining for soft drinks fling themselves over and under chairs.

To distract them the adults fold fliers about the Children of Prisoners Support Group into paper darts.

Eventually an officer shouts, 'Visitor for Cooke.'

You take a few steps forward. The officer steps close and whispers, 'First time, luv?'

You jump. He must be new. You turn away. The less he knows the better.

'Youse wanna go fer a beer after, luv?'

You cross your arms and shake your head. It's like visiting a foreign country.

'Be at the gate at four?'

You aren't that lonely.

'A bit long in the tooth for young Cooke, aren't youse, but?'

He's right about your preferring Gav, who wouldn't? You'd confided in each other every day like old friends. He'd had his first shot when he was twelve. He'd fetched beers for men who arrived when his mum still had someone with her. The day he gets out he's going to get a job in a gym. You trust him. Sort of.

'Visitor for Cooke, pro-ceed, please.'

A video camera is mounted at each turn in the corridor. A blue uniform opens the door and you scan the visiting area, willing Gav to be there, waiting. Visitors and prisoners sit hunched over tables like primary school parents at parent and teacher night. Not that you'd ever been to one, or were likely to go for that matter. A woman officer hands over the number nineteen and you wander among the tables looking for Gav.

'I don't care who the fuck he is, you didn't fuckin' hafta let him spend the night, did ya?'

A male voice. Nothing to do with you. Gav is wearing a white plastic bag with no opening in the front. A body bag.

'Table which?' You lip read him say to the female custodial officer. 'Nineteen? O-kay!'

He can't find the table with the nineteen on it because you're still clutching the number. You hope he isn't expecting someone more exciting. Finally he sees you.

'Hey, Chalkie. There's a table in the corner.'

What doesn't he want the officers to overhear? He wouldn't ask you to do anything illegal.

He unwinds your fingers from their grip on the number. You want him to keep touching them.

'Took a long while to get here, eh?'

'I've been here ages.'

'Me too.'

You smile and tell him about the police planting drugs on the baby.

'Tell me about having an addicted mum, eh? Talk quicker. We'll be lucky to get fifty minutes.'

He looks like he's been working out, but not using is the important thing.

'See Big Max's lady?' He points.

The whole room throbs. You turn in time to see Max's hand move under his lady's skirt. Probably she isn't wearing knickers. Gav says she tapes a sawn-off fit loaded with heroin to her thigh, a take-away for Max. Are drugs more a commodity than sex? You can never figure it out. That's Berko coughing, the one whose missus claims she got pregnant in this room. You cross your legs and check out what a toddler conceived during a jail visit looks like. Brown eyes, sticking-out ears, and sticking-up brown hair – just like Berko. The air, thick with volatilised juices, wraps around you like a body suit of sperm, sweat and sour breast milk. Thank goodness for cotton knickers.

You sit side by side at the low table next to layers of chipped mustard paint, craving a hit of passion, some touching, love — the things everyone else here seems to have in abundance.

You're desperate to hear him say something personal — like his release date has been brought forward, and he hasn't had a shot in months, and he's enrolled in a certificate in sports training, and he attributes all this to your excellent work. Just *I miss talking to you* would do.

'Instant coffee with fake milk and sugar?'

The legs of his chair scrape on the cement. Screams and swearing bounce off the high gloss walls. People intertwine like pretzels – hands down neckbands, hands under shirts, hands up skirts, hands down pants. Berko's clone, snot dripping from his nose, careens into the legs of your chair.

'This awful brew,' Gav places the coffee on the table.

You drain the last bitter drop and dig your right thumb nail into the bottom edge of the polystyrene until crescent-shaped dents ring the bottom, like the moon has orbited for the entirety of someone's lagging, one crescent for each month. He jiggles his legs.

Names are called out as new visitors replace those whose time is up. The crim at the next table leans over to tell Gav that, bad luck, a trannie with a stroller has been barred entry.

Was that redhead a trannie? Bringing in drugs?

'Gav, how's your course going?'

'It's impossible to study when you're two out. You know that.'

'But you're still submitting a unit every fortnight?'

'You try studying while you're locked up with some arsehole eighteen hours a day.'

'How many units have you sent in?'

'The guy I'm two-out with watches telly until three in the morning.'

Like you're responsible for the overcrowding. 'I suppose you've gone on request for earplugs?'

'No luck.'

He must have done something major to get the super offside.

'You bring some in. Give it a go, Chalk. Earplugs and packets of Drum. Not for me. For yourself. Prove to yourself you're no longer a puppet of the system.'

One earplug inside each cheek? Or in your ears and wear your hair down?

'I could end up in Mulawa.'

'Aw, don't be so middle class. You can count on me. I'd visit you.'

The hell he would! Suddenly it's quiet. The paint on the cement floor is worn so thin you see the grey underneath.

'Visitor for Cooke. One minute.'

Looking down puts you in touch with feelings, where you least want to go. He's looking straight ahead. You keep your chin level with the table, look into his dark smoky eyes. Pinned. Just like the rest of them. He won't even ring when he gets out.

'Doesn't matter, Chalk. I'm being sent to Goulburn tomorrow.'

'Goulburn. Why?'

'Visitor for Cooke, thirty seconds.'

You stand.

'If I'd been able to get enough tobacco I'd have come down easier, but you weren't here.'

'It's not my fault you're using,'

He stands up. 'Shh. Not my fault they urine-tested me when I least expected it.'

'Fuck.'

'Visit me in Goulburn, eh?'

'Time's up, Visitor for Cooke.'

'Please, Chalk?'

You touch cheeks.

Outside the gate the rain has stopped. Bright straw hats, striped bags and tee-shirts replace sandstone, brick and concrete. You join the queue at the ice cream vendor's cart. No sense feeling hungry at the beach.

Meant

'You'll be back.' He yanks the heavy metal gate open.

Predictable. But you're not going to let a screw's sarcasm get you. Not now. You stand your backpack up on the trolley, squat, grab it around the middle, lift it through the last gate. They said you'd be leaving first thing in the morning not after the lunchtime muster, but at least you're out and have the rest of your life ahead. Where the shadow of the sandstone wall ends, the pavement radiates heat. You can think of things you'd rather hug than a backpack. Keep your gob shut until the gate clanks. For the last time.

The backpack's heavy. Not like you're out of shape or anything. Never been in better nick. You hoist it up by the straps, attempt to swing it onto your shoulders. Good move you gave your telly to one of the cooks. Just after you'd gotten clean, he'd piled your plate with mashed spuds. That kind of friendship counted.

Rach is waiting outside some fish and chip shop she's crazy to visit. She's come up to take you back to Wollongong to live with her. Help you find the dole office when you get there. Maybe she'll cook a roast dinner to celebrate. That's what big sisters are for.

Lighten the load. You hope Chalkie isn't watching the books sail out of your hand and into the bin – level 2 English, the dictionary, *Streetwize* comics with emergency phone numbers, veggie maths, a history of your own people. No offence to her or the teachers. You transfer the squashed sandwiches and the bruised banana to an outside pocket of the pack. Just in case. Jump the backpack onto your shoulders and walk towards the road to Sydney. You have to cross four lanes of traffic to get to the bus stop. Whoever planted natives on the divider didn't bother to water them. There's still enough time to get to the dole office.

Bloody backpack.

You carried Kaila in the backpack when you were in Year 10 and she was almost one. As soon as the high school lunch bell rang, you'd sauntered across the playground, nipped behind the sheds, hurried across the dirt track next to the field and loped towards home. Skye's flat was home, the housing commission flats. Only a few k's from here. If Skye was awake you sneaked back to school in time for sixth period. If she wasn't, Kaila would need to be changed and fed. Carried in the backpack to the park. Skye was fourteen years older than you, old really, but, whatever. She didn't mother you or anything, and you cared for Kaila like she was your own daughter.

The bus shelter's roof is bashed in. No shade. The sun bounces off a couple of syringes on the paving around the side. You don't need them now, but your mates inside would give anything. The traffic whizzing past stirs the air around. Just as you lean over to pick up the fits a car swerves to the curb near the row of liver brick flats and skids to a stop, spraying gravel on the dried out nature strip. The driver's door opens and a bloke in a mustard tee-shirt gets out and checks a front tyre. Looks you over too. You're standing at a bus stop outside a jail, carrying everything you own. Your situation is tattooed all over your dark skin. You squint into the glare until the bloke slams the door and roars off. A freak out.

The traffic flies by, streaks of red and white, yellow and white, puke green. Sweat's running down the back of your neck. He might not have been after anything. Maybe you should've gone over to the car. Asked for a lift. You pay out for never being friendly enough. Or you save yourself. Hard to know. Leave the fits for someone who needs them. Bat the flies away.

Almost three hours before the appointment. Nothing between you and the dole office but the two buses and train to the Gong. Rach'll take you to the pub after, introduce you around. The bus when it finally pulls up is packed with kids in school uniforms. Must be on an excursion. You get on anyway. Only going a couple of stops. Kaila's five now, in kindy.

How long since you felt air-conditioning?

You took two stairs at a time when you heard Kaila crying, turned the key, picked her up from the drawer she slept in. She was eight weeks old when you moved in. You learned to wash the bottle and heat the milk fast to stop the crying. Often by the time Skye got out of bed and took the baby with her to score, it was too late to sneak back to school.

A boy in school uniform sitting on the bus seat next to you gets up and stands in the aisle. Stares at the tatts on your arms. Your legs. You're a leper. Scum. But Kaila wouldn't be afraid, she'll remember the way you took care of her.

You remember walking to school. Kindy. *When everyone sits down we'll have a story. We are all waiting for you, Gavin.* You liked the story about the Scottie dog. Maybe the cats in Scotland came in funny shapes too. Scottie cats? Suppose Kaila asked you things like that? Skye'd say, *How the fuck would I know what fuckin' cats look like in fuckin' Scotland?*

On the footpath a man in shorts leads a little girl by the hand. Her father? Grandpa? A pervert? Who could tell? You sent Kaila a card with the release date printed in big letters. Drew a picture of the two of you carrying fishing poles like cartoon Kooris carrying spears. She always laughed at your jokes. Kids don't forget.

You check the directions on the piece of paper and get off the bus near the fish and chip shop. Rach said she'd be early. Maybe she came earlier. Or her train's late.

Don't look over your shoulder to check who's staring. Don't turn around and don't look down. Focus on the picture painted

                                PERMISSION TO LIE

on the shop window – a blue fish with a bloodshot eye and twisted lips. Too many hooks. Poor bloody fish.

An hour of freedom wasted at bus stops. You go into the shop, the only shop within sight, and buy a bag of chips. Not bad. You sit on one of the benches outside sucking petrol fumes and chip fat. Of all the places to meet in Sydney, why did Rach pick this spot? Must've scored here or something. Should have insisted on meeting at the Country Trains Platform.

Don't look down or you'll get into feelings. Look straight ahead, chin level with the ground the way the jail psych taught in NLP. Neu-ro Lin-guis-tic Pro-gram-ming taught you a thing or two. Handy to check out what others are thinking. If they're looking high left they're lying, high right and they're imagining or remembering. When the psych with the shiny clean-shaven cheeks said to visualise the colour of the first house you lived in, you lied. Everyone else in the group had lived in a house. You *had* to lie.

A skinny guy is sitting opposite you under the window of the fish and chips. Teeth missing. Pumpkin grin all over his dial.

You lower the pack to the ground, face the other way, run your fingers through the number two clip the do-gooder nun gave you. Too short. It's like everyone can read what you're thinking, a cartoon bubble floating over your skull. You have questions ready to ask Rach if she shows up. Is NLP just a con job for shrinks to get their fingers into someone's brains?

A bus stops four lanes across the road and two chicks get off. Shame their skirts aren't shorter. Sensational legs. One has curly brown hair, thick glasses, long long legs. Last time you saw her, Rach's hair was pulled back, a ratty fringe attempting to disguise how craggy her face looked. Probably she'd wear sunnies and a peaked cap. Might even bring a spare cap she'd picked up at St Vinnies for fifty cents. You take out a scrap of paper and add – *NLP common knowledge?* Everyone must recognise a junkie who's just gotten out. Probably looking for track marks. But everyone has them. Everyone who's shot up with a communal fit sharpened on paving. You could have rinsed those fits in vinegar from the chips.

Several people stand near the entrance to some medical offices, smoking. A woman hurries outside, down the steps, flicks a yellow plastic lighter. She smokes a tailor-made in three breaths. What a waste. She scrubs the sole of her shoe on the pavement to crush the life out of the butt, and pivots to go back inside fast. Needs a chill pill. You'd learned to make every drag last, then given it up in seggro. The skinny guy definitely is eyeing you over.

In one of the exercises you were supposed to visualise a person you were scared of. The psych said, *now picture this person a little shorter than you, then shrink him to knee high. Look down at the top of his head, move him closer.* You pictured the smart ass crim in the weights yard. You made him drop the weights, wiped the sneer off his ugly face, then scooted him around like something in a video game. *Dress him in something ugly.* You snort when you remember the bubblegum pink dressing gown, his hand holding the toilet brush, cover your nose and mouth with your hand too late to muffle the noise. When the psych asked you to do the exercise again, you shrank Dad, tied an apron around his gut, added oven mitts. *Do this if someone is giving you a hard time,* the psych had said. *Don't give them the satisfaction of seeing your anger. You don't even have to speak.* Maybe NLP has its uses. You didn't tell the psych anything he hadn't already read in the report with your name on the top.

The heat is rising from the street in dry waves. Another bus pulls up. No peaked cap gets off. No Rach. The skinny guy pulls out a packet of Drum.

The Parole Board is cool about you living at her flat. You know fuck all about Wollongong which is a good thing. No fear of running into old dealers, or junkies who think you owe them, no fear about Skye getting you to score. No history at the dole office or the cop station. But you'd rather stay in Sydney to see Kaila.

'Mate?' the skinny guy on the bench calls out. He extends the hand holding the packet.

Rach mentioned a job in the kitchen of the pub where she works. Can't be worse than the jail kitchen. If you can work for a screw you can work for anyone.

You'd lost the kitchen job for calling the screwess a clueless lardy cunt. Earned a week in seggro. One side of the zoo cage was metal bars, with most of the paint scraped off. The other sides were sandstone covered in layers of ice blue paint. Paint so thick you couldn't read the carved messages. You wouldn't forget the stainless steel crapper without a seat or lid set smack in the middle of the cage, facing into the corridor. With your habit, having a shit took a week. The welfare worker and one of the teachers had turned their faces away when they walked by, but the screws, even the women, gawked. Screaming obscenities won you more days in the slammer.

How were you supposed to get dope when you never saw another crim? You'd had to stop using. Then they had nothing to hold over you. Withdrawal gave you the shits, same as it always did, but also choices.

A mutt darts from behind the fish and chip shop, between the parked cars, into the traffic. Brakes screech. Yelps rise above the honking, the crash of metal. The skinny guy stares at you. You shrug. Kaila's still too young to be allowed to cross streets alone.

In seggro your stomach cramped-up, eyes, nose and guts streamed, and your head ached so bad you never thought of correspondence courses, let alone exams. Then Chalkie brought the exams down to your cage. She wouldn't start timing until you had a table and chair.

'He can sit on the crapper,' a screw said.

Chalkie said examination conditions meant a desk or table and a chair.

'Who's responsible if fuckface here decides to heave furniture?'

'I'll phone the Ombudsman and ask?' Chalkie said, all snide.

It'd taken two screws to edge a park bench into your cage. As if you were a maniac. As if you wanted to heave furniture. You hadn't wanted to, that was the thing. You just wanted to pass the exams. To learn. To excel. You liked the feel of the word in your mouth. Excel. The way the tip of your tongue flicked the roof of your mouth. Excel. Excellent. That's exactly what you wanted. And they've gone and made you chuck all the books in the bin. Fucking cunts. Hardly your fault if no one picks you up.

As the skinny bloke approaches, his pumpkin head flickers. The sun touching his cheekbone or something. Your hand reaches for the Drum.

A quick look to see if big sis is shimmering through the waves of heat. Nope. Only twenty minutes before the train leaves. Then you would have had an hour and a half with nothing to do but stare at the talent. Where the fuck is Rach, anyway? Not the first time she's let you down. Once something like this happens it's always the same. There's no moving on. It's meant.

It was meant that winter afternoon when Skye first let you snort her smack. You both thought so. You can bunk at her place if Rach doesn't show. See if the kid remembers you this time. Just one hit would be a bit of all right. The Parole Board doesn't have to know everything.

The pumpkin head flickers again, brighter this time.

Unaccompanied

Robyn's holiday began the moment she clicked the seat belt together. Too late to worry about what she might have forgotten to pack.

'Ladies and gentlemen and young ladies and gentlemen, this short video refreshes the minds of even our most sophisticated travellers about how to slip into one of our designer life jackets in the unlikely event of an emergency. We sincerely hope there will be no emergencies this morning. Your crew has just flown in to Sydney from Perth so you can imagine how tired we all are. Only joking! Just don't push your luck with our patience. And please remain seated as long as … '

These young people had a different concept of service. Luckily it was a short flight. A seat belt buckle thumped her stomach.

'Sorry, lady.'

The boy in the window seat looked as though he might be seven-ish. He stood up. Why was he standing just when they were about to take off? She never understood children. He galumphed over her legs, his heels rasping her shins, laddering her pantihose. He bounded over the empty seat and stood in the aisle. Robyn blamed herself. She'd broken her never-fly-during-school-holidays rule. The boy turned back toward Robyn and leered into her face. His runny nose almost touched hers. He didn't seem to want anything except attention.

'Sit down and fasten your seat belt so we can take off,' she said, fossicking in her bag for a tissue. She undid her seatbelt and stood up to let him pass.

The boy blew his nose, handed her back the tissue, then stared out the window.

'Put it in the pocket of your shorts.'

As soon as the seat belt sign went off and the captain had finished reading his welcome ladies and gentlemen, young ladies and gentlemen message, the boy resumed fidgeting. He kicked off the dirty thongs.

'I'm bored.'

'Are your parents here?' Perhaps they would have an empty seat close to them. He crawled over her legs, and stood in the aisle.

'No. I'm bored.'

'Don't you have something to do? A book?'

Robyn thought flight attendants must be accustomed to coping with unaccompanied children. This child was not her problem. The flight attendant was offering pillows but you had to pay to borrow them.

'Excuse me? Miss? This child needs something to do.'

'Not to worry. It's no trouble fetching an entertainment pack. Eleven dollars ninety-five.'

Not to worry? What a thing to say. 'He needs something to keep him entertained. He doesn't belong to me.'

The boy is coaxed back into his seat but refuses to fasten his seat belt even loosely until he is given an entertainment pack.

'I'm not paying twelve dollars. Isn't there something you can give him to do?'

'Not unless you pay for it.'

'Why should I pay? I don't even know him.'

'I'm ADHD,' he said. 'Frequent flier.'

Robyn wasn't wasting twelve dollars on a hyperactive brat.

She'd been looking forward to reading a collection of Alice Munro's short stories she'd ordered especially from the library. In normal circumstances short stories were perfect for travelling. Since this wasn't a normal circumstance, she opened the in-flight magazine. A small hand grabbed for it.

'Let go. You have your own copy.'

She flipped through the pictures of seafood platters at tropical paradises, searching for comics or puzzles. What's your name?'

'I told you already, A-D-E-Y, pronounced, A-DEE.'

'Let go, Adey. Your copy of the magazine seems to be missing, unfortunately.'

'What's your name?'

'My friends call me Robyn. Here, borrow mine.'

'It's not yours; it's the airlines, and I've done all the puzzles. I'm a frequent flier.'

She found geometric spaces in the pictures of paradise where the boy could write his name. She helped him start with large As and taper to tiny Ys in the triangles. 'See this square? Fit a square-shaped Adey into it.' Adey in a circular beach umbrella, an oval, a rectangle, a parallelogram, a trapezoid. They were defacing page after page of the magazine she always took care to leave uncreased for the next passenger, but it served Virgin Airlines right. She could be child phobic. Lots of people were. Her hairdresser charged more to trim a child's hair than an adult's to encourage mothers to take their nitty offspring elsewhere.

The flight attendant, Vivi, stopped the food and drinks trolley two seats in front of them. Robyn curtly refused to order a cuppa for herself because she would have to buy something for the boy. Something loaded with sugar that would probably make him wriggle more than he already was wriggling. The airlines had no right to seat her next to a demanding unaccompanied child just because she was travelling solo. In her head she was already composing a letter to the travel section of the *Herald*.

Just recently she'd read an article that claimed the biggest improvement the public, well those who participated in the survey, wanted on planes was to seat families separately from adults travelling without children. The article said a separate area for children was more important than the width of the seats or the amount of legroom. At the time she had queried the reliability of the survey. She was surprised that people weren't more concerned about legroom.

Legroom wasn't so important on the short flight to Brisbane. People chose this flight because it was cheap. No one preferred to take off at six-thirty in the morning. Who had gelled his hair and delivered him to the airport by five-thirty?

'What's my reward?' he demanded.

'You need to be rewarded for printing your own name?'

'Un huh.'

'You have the window seat.'

'I always have the window seat. Frequent flier. My dad says broads who have their boobs hanging out are sluts.'

Attention-getting comments were best ignored. Maybe he was referring to the flight attendant. Certainly not Robyn herself. Next time *she* would book a window seat. This generation of children were taught to be selective and all of them wanted a window seat. She would never repeat the mistake of flying during school holidays. Nor would she fly Virgin again. If only Qantas were a competitive price. A Qantas flight attendant would be older and more willing to assume responsibility. Robyn's glasses careened half way off the bridge of her nose. The magazine landed on her arm.

'Sorry lady.'

'Now look what's happened.' Air disaster! And of course the sleep-deprived Virgin was nowhere in sight. Probably napping. Robyn's nose stopped bleeding before she could find another tissue. Her multifocals weren't broken, thank goodness. She'd have hated to spend her whole holiday visiting a Brisbane optometrist's shop. Thank goodness she had decided not to go to Cambodia or she'd have gone crazy on the long flight.

One thing was certain. No child with ADHD was going to get her chocolate bars. After the plane did its emergency landing on the sea, after she slid down the chute to the life raft shoeless, when the blow-up vests were all inflated and manually topped up, when everyone had tested their little light and whistle, when they had found the oars and decided the direction in which to row, and elected someone to take charge, when they had somehow managed while bailing the dingy to catch a small fish, and everyone else was sawing chunks off it with a shell, and sharks and cannibals were lurking, she would have three bars of dark chocolate laced with slivers of orange for sustenance and the prevention of scurvy.

'Someone meeting you in Brisbane?' she asked him.

'Mum. At sixteen hundred-thirty when she gets off her shift.'

'What time's that? Four-thirty? That's a long while to wait! What will you do until then?'

'Hang out with the old planespotters watching the 747s take off and land, same's I always do. I'm hungry.'

An article she'd read in the *Sydney Morning Herald* found a direct correlation between the number of people sharing a meal and the amount of food they consumed. People who eat alone eat least. She was thin, too thin; probably there was some truth in it. And now, she suddenly was hungry although she'd microwaved the same quarter cup of porridge with skim milk the way she always did, just earlier. It was the boy's fault. Like the young women living together when she'd been studying nursing falling into menstrual synch, she was falling into hunger synch. Pheromones had a lot to answer for, she was well aware of that, but it couldn't be pheromones with a young boy. Maybe she had just gotten up too early.

'Who's picking *you* up?' he thumped her wrist.

Planespotters? She was too busy counting on her fingers the number of hours the boy would be by himself in an airport to say she was going to a guest house in a wilderness park where she'd go on guided bird walks. Someone should notify child welfare, a child left to his own devices for eight hours.

'I'm hungry.'

'Stop kicking. Who put you on the plane?'

'My Dad. He lives a long way from the airport. In Parklea.'

Probably in one of those trailer parks next to the prison. 'So you had to get up very early?' She'd gotten up at four-thirty and she lived in Stanmore, not all that far from Mascot.

'Yup, have you any chocolate?'

'Your Dad must pack things for you to eat as well as things to do.'

'You know my Dad?'

'No.'

'Well, if you knew him you'd know his girlfriend has twins besides being preggers. The slut has so much to keep her busy she's useless.'

Robyn rummaged in her handbag. She broke the chocolate bar in half.

'Make it last and don't talk like that. She might be your stepmother someday.'

'Ever read *Bluebeard?* Ladies always give me chocolate but intense orange is not my very favourite.'

She chewed and swallowed quickly, before she had time to savour its smoothness. The bitter citrus flavour lingered.

'What is your favourite?'

'Reese's chocolate-covered peanut butter cups.'

'I don't have any peanut butter.' She was relieved he hadn't said something about Bluebeard leaving naked ladies to drip on meat hooks. Her memory of the story was hazy but she still felt uncomfortable about rooms with red floors.

'I'm not allowed to take peanut butter to school. If someone with anaphylaxis has even the teeny tiniest taste they would have to be stabbed with the epi-pen. Orange chocolate is my second favourite.'

How open he is. She wished she had sandwiches she could give him to eat in the airport while he waited for his mother. At the wilderness park meals were included in the package. One year, when they'd placed her at a communal table, she'd met a grandmother and her granddaughter. The woman confided that each grandchild was invited to accompany her to the guest house the year the child turned eight. The year each turned fourteen they were invited to accompany her to London for the Easter holidays. Robyn thought it could be an extremely civilised arrangement, if you were rich. And had grandchildren, of course.

From under his seat the boy brought out a notebook. 'I only show this to people who share their chocolate.'

Adey nudges her arm with the corner of his notebook.

She can't help looking at the picture of his mother in her nurse's aide uniform, then his truck driver father in a peaked cap.

She had wanted to be a parent but it had never happened. The man she'd secretly wanted to marry was conscripted to DaNang and came back a changed person.

The boy showed her a snap of his father's girlfriend smoking in a bikini, the two-year-old twins fighting over a hose. Apparently his own mother was single with no other children.

'Is this a photo of your Mum's mother, your grandmother?' She had wanted grandchildren desperately, far more than she had ever wanted children.

'Nanna's dead. That's Jean.'

When Robyn was younger she'd called Barnardo's to enquire about fostering a little girl. She even went to an information session. She'd pictured herself shopping in David Jones for fairy wings, a toy tea set, sheets with pink stripes. She imagined taking her foster daughter to see the ballet, when she could afford it.

But the agencies always refused to separate siblings. She agreed it was important to keep siblings together, but she couldn't manage more than one child; her unit and her life weren't big enough. How could she look after the whole dysfunctional family of someone who was in a psychiatric ward or a jail cell?

How could she be guaranteed she wouldn't be given the kind of children who would slit her throat when she was asleep?

 PERMISSION TO LIE

After she read in the *Herald* about a woman who was jailed for stabbing her foster mother, Robyn arranged to sponsor a girl in Eritrea.

'Is that a photo of your Dad's mother?'

'Dad hasn't spoken to her since she dobbed.'

'Who's this then?'

'That's Carol.'

'She looks nice. Well groomed. This one?'

'Ruthie. She sends me postcards. That's Dot.'

'Your aunties?'

'No. Guess. That's the birthday card man.'

'Baby sitters?'

'No. Bob's a miner from Mt Isa. He plays the harmonica.'

'Neighbours?'

'On planes and in airports. Any more chocolate?'

'Morning tea time.' She breaks the second bar in two, hands him half and nibbles hers. Adey will know the best place in the airport to have lunch. 'Are you going to introduce me to your Mum?'

LOST FERR

Wearing clothes is not compulsory

I woke up wheezing, covered in sweat. Inside the van wisps floated, as though some animal were moulting. I'd spent the night in Len's van, under his picnic rug. Dog hair, cat hair, feathers, anything could be on this rug. Or maybe his sleeping bag was filled with down. Breathing shallowly, being unable to take a deep breath, had always made me panicky. I was with a man I hardly knew, who had never seen my body in a nightgown or a bathing suit, much less nude. Weird that he hadn't come on to me. It was as if this was the dress rehearsal he wasn't quite ready for, perhaps with a different female lead. I had hoped something would happen. Better than sitting home alone anyway.

If I were totally honest I'd have to admit that I always read the singles columns, even when I was still married. A month or two earlier I'd checked out the ads for singles functions in the Saturday *Herald* with a fresh perspective. I wanted the universe to send me a single available man who was interested in the arts, definitely someone with an income and without a lot of baggage. Not all arty people were on the dole. My ex was arty and employed. Worse luck that he'd taken his assets with him. If only I had thought about the future earlier. Every time I'd suspected his attention – or his body – had gone wandering I should have raced to the art supply shop with his credit card.

I arranged the ads I'd cut out on the table, crumpled up those where the woman's age or racial background were mentioned, or where offspring were part of the package. Parents Without Partners. Definitely not interested. Only a bridge group and a bushwalking group survived my cull. Bridge was out unless

I wanted to renew my relationship with tobacco. And my grandparents played bridge. Bushwalking was cheap and, even if I didn't meet a man, at least I'd get fit. A fit single sounded better than a single smoker, a bit like a merry widow. Lucky widows. They inherited everything and never had to move out of their homes. But it would be selfish to wish the rover dead, just because he could afford to live in the house and I couldn't.

At my first meeting with the bushwalkers an athletic-looking maths teacher, a designer of web sites, and someone who organised occupational health and safety courses for hospital staff welcomed me and introduced themselves. These women – all stunning – said the men would like me because I was short.

The mathematician said, 'And Stephanie wears skirts.'

The club organiser, the man whose flat we were in, took one look at my high heels and said, 'Look for a capital E on legs. That's the Grade: EASY icon in the newsletter.'

Duh. All I had to do was read the newsletter and book an event. It wouldn't be too challenging because I did my own housework, stretched my own canvases and stood up to paint.

One night, shortly after that, I was feeling good, surrounded by sinewy super-fit men, standing on the back veranda of a bushwalker's terrace house, admiring the view of the Anzac Bridge with the city lights in the distance. I was sipping Riesling (so eighties), trying not to think about cigarettes, when one of the men mentioned he'd been swimming and someone else, maybe Len, muttered something about liking the feel of water against his body without having swimmers on. I mentally peeled off their tee-shirts, only half hearing their conversation over the dance music and the clatter of the dishwasher. Perhaps I smiled or nodded. From then on Len seemed to make an effort to get to know me.

He phoned to invite me to join a walk he was leading. *Royal National Park, Maximum of twelve, Grade: EASY, Book early*, the newsletter had said. But he was the only one to show up at the

   PERMISSION TO LIE

meeting place, a dock. Why hadn't anyone else signed up? He worked with families who kept their kids home from school, something about attendance. Must have had police clearance to work with kids. He led me along a beach and up a path onto the headland, pointed out the intersection of Port Hacking, Bate Bay and the Tasman. We examined outlines carved in sandstone where Aborigines had watched whales, sharks, turtles and fish swim by.

'The carvings are like newsletter headlines, *Best fishing here!*'

He knew the Latin names of the gums, wattles, paper barks and grevilleas we passed and where to find waratahs and Gymea lilies. He knew where to see deer. He knew everything.

'I talk too much when I'm nervous,' he said.

I was satiated with information and ready for a break before the first hour was up but I wasn't scared of him.

'You're adventurous so you won't mind this.' He expected me to shimmy along a narrow sandstone cliff face, with the sea bashing the rocks below. Creeping along the narrow ledge made me more desperate for a cigarette than any game of bridge.

'You OK?' He held out his hand.

Len asked me to go with him to try out a walking track he was supposed to write up for the newsletter. I'd imagined we'd stay in the kind of guesthouse where a pianist played cocktail music before dinner. He'd said, Southern Highlands. But yesterday he spotted the name of a mountain on the map. He said it'd be fun to climb it, even though the road we'd have to drive down to get to the valley looked as twisty as five-minute noodles. I lied when I said I was happy to climb the mountain.

It was already late when the van started up a throaty protest but Len continued to navigate the bends in the steep, dirt road. The throatiness became hoarseness. He said it sounded like the muffler was scraping on the track. He needed to get underneath and have a look before we could drive up again. At the bottom of the track, by torchlight, we could just read the sign.

WELCOME ADULTS!

WEARING CLOTHES IS NOT COMPULSORY
YOUR RIGHT NOT TO WEAR CLOTHING IS
RESPECTED

TRACK CLOSED 6 PM UNTIL 6 AM.

A nudist colony! Thank goodness I wasn't by myself. He said there was a mattress in the back of the van and it was good I was the adventurous sort. Oh yeah. The most adventurous thing I'd ever done was draw a nude model. What an idiot to have brought a negligee.

In the morning light I unpeeled the picnic rug, liberating more of the allergens. I didn't care if my sneezing woke him. I was so short of tissues I had to find a place to hang them up. I draped my towel around my shoulders.

Outside, a creek and a ghost gum provided a foreground to the mountain: a triangle of searing raw meat against a sky of lavender. I put on my sunnies.

Len offered me his handkerchief, towel and antihistamine pills. I accepted everything. He glanced away while I wrapped his towel around my waist. He was whistling in Birkenstocks and a towelling hat as he left the van to hike up to the camp shop to pay the fees and buy me tissues. I buckled on my paint-spattered sandals and tagged along to see what he was up to. You'd have thought by now that I'd have bought hiking boots, or at least trainers, but I wanted to be sure I really needed them. At the general store I selected groceries while Len read the postcards sent by nudist camp members, looked at the snaps on the bulletin board, and read the comments in the visitors' book. He attempted to further ingratiate himself by asking

Permission To Lie

embarrassing questions about the people in the photos. As he packed the groceries, Rawhide Ray asked me how I was settling in.

'Can't wait to climb that mountain.'

I wanted to ask him how he managed without pockets. He smirked, probably stripping off my towels with his eyes. I visually stripped away the shop counter he was standing behind. About ten years older than Len, who must have been at least five years older than me. Len's age was a forbidden topic. If I'd asked, I'd have given him permission to lie. Allowing him to lie the first time gave him permission to lie again. I'd been there. Once was enough.

After breakfast he disappeared under the van and I set out for a walk with my sketchbook. Brambles encrusted with dried blackberries blocked access to the creek where dirty white threads and globules clung to rocks. The dirt path ended at a razor wire fence where the creek continued to dribble away from the factory upstream. I trudged up toward the camp's swimming pool. Caravans were everywhere, their fenced gardens choked with vines, their screened patios crammed with plastic picnic settings. A woman stood up from her weeding, pushed the fringe off her sweaty forehead and asked if we were settling in OK. Her withered breasts dangled. Clutching the towels, I told her how nice it was to be in an unspoilt environment.

'Things liven up on Saturday nights. You and your bloke must come to our barbecue. Near the pool. At dusk.'

The chlorine fumes, when I got close, reminded me of the indoor pool near the station where I'd had swimming lessons when I was a kid. What a funny thing to get nostalgic about. No one was around but I didn't risk a dip.

Even when I was a child I was wary of nudist camps.

'Wrap Gran's present, Stephanie,' Mummy had yelled down the stairs and I'd run to the old desk. One of her drawers was chockablock with wrapping paper, tags and ribbons. After

I bundled up Gran's gift, I peeked in the third drawer from the bottom – Daddy's drawer. Opening it was forbidden. I opened it further, and peeled back the tape sealing a tan envelope. The calendar I pulled out showed a photo of a suntanned family I'd never seen. Starkers. Playing ball under trees hung with dangling brown fruit and yucky brown leaves. My finger brushed the nudies by mistake. Then I deliberately traced around each, even the man. I tore half the page off its spiral binding and bent it so their bodies rubbed against each other. After I kissed their boobies and willies, I scrubbed my hands and mouth but I still felt like chucking. I hoped Mummy wouldn't look at me and guess what I'd done.

The red mountain, the periwinkle sky, the white tree trunk, the turquoise pool – an improvement on sepia. I wished I could take my lungs out, rinse them in pure water, wring them dry and put them back. Then sluice away the embarrassment. Artists weren't supposed to suffer from embarrassment.

I was attempting to hose the grass and leaves off my feet when four people approached Len's van. I scrambled inside and closed the back door quickly. Two rapid knocks. Before I'd adjusted the towels again, the side door slid open with a metallic whirring sound. I knelt facing two couples, as dark and wrinkled as smoked fish.

'How're you settling in?' the kippers chanted.

Len spread his sleeping bag and rug on the dirt.

'Couples are especially welcome,' said one of the women, staring at Len as she spread her towel on his sleeping bag.

'Couples who are seriously interested,' the second woman sat down.

'We offer the cream the opportunity to buy an on-site van, on the rare occasion when one becomes available,' the scrawnier man cut in, scratching an insect bite.

Len didn't lower his eyes from the faces. I wondered which woman was with which man.

'We like what we've seen of you,' said the last man.

We like what we've seen! Talk about tactless pervs. Were they bored swingers in search of new partners? A breed fearing extinction? Investment heavy, cash poor?

'Three vans are available with foundations and annexes.' The less scrawny man pointed out caravans covered in choko vines. 'If you would like to inspect them.' He seemed to edge his hand towards my bare knee. 'You have to stay for at least three weeks before you apply with the deposit. There are no restrictions about the way the days are grouped, no restrictions at all. We're good about that, leave it all up to you.'

The first woman interrupted, 'Don't forget, people without partners.'

The less scrawny man sighed, 'A bloke must always be accompanied by his better half but we never ask to see proof of anything. We're good about that.' He sighed again.

'No offence intended, but no female cats on heat either,' the first woman said. 'Unfortunate incidents have forced us.' After a pause, she turned toward Len, 'How'd you find out about us?'

I crumpled desiccated gum leaves. Over the noise of the cicadas Len was nervously droning on about some woman named Janet who'd stayed here. He even made up dates. If he was anxious to get rid of the kippers because he wanted to climb the mountain, he concealed it well. I stood up as best I could while grasping towels – my signal for them to stand and leave. They didn't take the hint. Len tossed me the matches and nodded toward the gas jet. I lit it and found the tea bags. While the water was coming to a boil I thought about the sepia calendar. I'd replaced it in its envelope, certain that the next summer Mummy'd insist on going to the beach as usual. If Daddy said, *You won't need all those clothes where we're going,* that'd be the sign for me to run away.

'It's only decent to go to their barbie,' Len said after one of the men helped him repair the muffler. 'A few drinks and a sausage sizzle, then a dip, if we feel like staying that long.'

I was almost as eager to roll up for a nudist barbie as I had been to gallop up a mountain. He dragged me up a path where petrochemical fumes frizzed up to meet dripping fat. Len paid for us both and pulled open tinnies. No barbecue aprons and chef's hats for this crowd. They were as brown as the bangers and HP sauce. We were as white as the sliced bread.

Len stared at faces untouched by sunscreen, at ropy necks, at veins on hands wrapped around tinnies. Everyone was drinking. At the same time Ray knocked over his tinnie, he offered me a snag stuck on the end of a three-pronged fork. Never thought of Neptune as a prick before.

When it was dark and everyone was still busy eating and drinking, I slipped away to the unlit pool, left the towels at the far rim, dipped underwater to sluice the sweat and dust off, lay back and floated, studying the stars. Suddenly spotlights blazed on and I heard shouting, felt turbulence, splashes.

'Who does she think she is, eh?'

'Think you're too good to mix with us, eh?'

I panicked when brown arms reached out, grabbing, toward me, splashing, closing in, 'C'mere, come mere!'

Len jumped into the pool. I thrashed into the splash, towards him, away from the dark clutching hands.

'No! Go away, go away,' I yelled, and then Len blocked them, shielded me to the edge. We scrambled out together. I heard their cackling as we sprinted, past the fireplace where logs were burning and more spotlights came on, and everywhere we ran, more spotlights and macabre laughter. We raced back barefoot, towel-less and panting, to the cab of his van and locked ourselves in. I only dropped his hand when he wrapped his shirt around my shoulders.

'Thanks.'

He started the motor. 'No one's following; it'll be okay,' he said, gunning it, past the shop while I crouched low. Gravel rolled away behind us. He flicked on the headlights and drove up the steep dirt track, red dust billowing behind the taillights. We twisted around bend after bend, with my oil pastels rattling in my case and his expectations – whatever they were – still unspoken.

'Thanks, Len,' I broke the silence

'I think they were jealous.'

He was okay. Lean and fit. Who knew block out cream could be a turn on? When the track levelled out, I asked him, 'Why did we come here?'

'Remember I asked about Janet? My birth mum. Been trying to find her.'

'In a nudist camp?'

'Janet's last address was a camping ground and I'd visited all the others.'

'And the kippers wouldn't let you visit without a chaperone?'

'Right.'

'Find out anything?'

'No one had heard of her.'

'Maybe she ran away too.'

'Maybe she did.' He had a nice warm laugh. 'I should've just told you but I was afraid you'd refuse.'

We pulled over and dressed before we reached the highway.

Back home I prime my largest canvas, and, with adventurous brush strokes, paint a lavender background, a red triangle.

Pentimento with fog

Stephanie

He's having an *in absentia* relationship with his birth mother. Totally preoccupied, and with as much animal magnetism as a sincere wombat. He's sweet though, the way he sort of rescued me. And good looking, if you can see beyond the baggy Kathmandu walking shorts and the strine hat. The day after we got home from the valley I took myself off to the mall and bought Dunlop Volleys in anticipation. Mum always said you won't meet anyone by staying at home, better to be out there, doing. He is a decent bloke. A start.

Len

Bought a new sound system and scrubbed the grout between the tiles with a toothbrush the last time a woman came here. The smears of lipstick on the wine glass and coffee mug were the last I saw of her. Inviting any woman home is risky, but particularly an artistic woman like Stephanie. She mentioned French doors off the dining room and a studio. Not exactly a two-bed red brick unit. Best not contaminate this place with bad memories, best keep it just for myself, in case things don't work out.

I deleted dozens of e-mails from strangers saying, *wish I could help you find your birth mother, Len*. Now all that's in the past. I'm trashing everything about the search for Janet, except the last letter and the photo.

As part of my clean-up I piled all the camping equipment in one corner of the junk room and hung my sleeping bag over the top of a door to air. That would be another thing about having Stephanie here. She's allergic to down. You don't need a doona in this weather, but how interested is she? *Should I buy synthetic pillows?* That would put it straight on the line. A good sort would say, *Come over to my place,* or *I'll bring my own pillow.*

Stephanie

Len must have left a message on someone else's answering machine, or had a computer crash. Maybe his letter was caught in a fold of a postie's bag, like that woman in the newspaper who received her false teeth back decades after the dentist had mailed them. Ha. Len wouldn't be bothered with snail mail. Only it's not funny. Maybe an ex-lover was sitting on his doorstep when he'd pulled up Sunday night in his van. Or he could be caught up with work. But how demanding could that be, a social worker getting kids to go to school?

I started a painting about the problem of integrating foreground and background. Letters and numbers stencilled onto the canvas will represent lost words, disconnections. The container of primer smelled foul, the rags mouldy. A cockroach crawled along the shelf. The dog next door barked all day. And that fucking car alarm!

I replayed the incidents from the weekend in the valley for the umpteenth time. Imagined how my dad might brag to Len about his compost heap while Len explained the wonders of a Bokashi bin. Then I phoned Kristy.

'Let him miss you.'

I went out at the times he was most likely to ring and stayed overnight at her place in Paddington. Did a gallery crawl. Checked that there were no freak accidents or obits reported in *Bushwalking Singles,* then shredded it and collaged the strips onto the canvas.

Talk about cool, he phoned three whole weeks later. My attempt to outdo his nonchalance was feeble.

'Gallery openings, films, dinners with friends.' Nothing gender specific.

'I'm leading the bushwalk at Bouddi. Thought you might want to come.'

I didn't want to be part of any group he was leading. I wanted to see him alone or not at all. I tried to picture him in a restaurant by candlelight – the hiking boots, those shorts with the pouches at the sides, the towelling hat covering his bald spot. Not likely. The sun would set while we drank lukewarm tins of beer in his van, followed by dinner at the RSL or bowling club on main street. 'A walk, just us, Saturday arvo?' I asked.

Len

In the inner west I was always driving past places I knew too much about. If the place didn't remind me of trying to find Janet, it reminded me of the kids I was supposed to get back to school. Stories followed me home, crept into my van, even on bushwalks. I was obsessed with pointing out too much to the people I was giving a lift to. See the shopping trolleys in front of that terrace? The kid who lived there had nits so bad he spent a fortnight in hospital. See the townhouse with the mattress flopped against the fence and the keyhole of the front door only a metre off the ground? Those kids started shooting up when they were ten. See that flat? A five-year-old flicked matches on that carpet. See that kid? A boy frocked up in his sister's dress.

A relief to catch public transport. Take a bus to Central and catch a train to the Mountains. Katoomba may have more than its share of sad stories but they're not my responsibility. If I pack groceries I can avoid having to go to a supermarket where I'm sure to see a woman with a screamer on her hip blowing the child allowance on ciggies. No need to go on about it. I don't want Stephanie to suspect I'm a burnt-out do-gooder. Judgemental as well.

Sometimes I feel like rescuing the kids I work with from their parents, parents who shoot up or empty the bottle; of course they make me wonder about my birth mum. What kind of hell would my childhood have been if she'd been like that?

What made her give me away? She must have been one gutsy dame. Only someone tough could give a child away. Not me.

Stephanie

Saturday at the Bay Run the grit and pollen swirled into my eyes whenever I took my sunnies off. On the hill between the bridge and Callan Park I turned into the wind to blow the hair off my face, catching as much as possible in a pony tail, anchoring the rest with clips, to keep the wiry strands off my swollen nose. The haircut a total waste. Every November the pollen made my sinuses swell and my head ache. He walked on ahead, toward the carvings in the sandstone, rabbiting on about how everything these days had to be paved or fenced. He hated the Iron Cove Bridge with its metal stairs. He hated guardrails.

'How old were you when you started bushwalking, Len?'

'An Indian brave in moccasins, imagining my Kid Care Auntie was a deer disappearing around a bend in her brown plaid skirt. We'd catch the bus to do some errand in Katoomba and hike back to her place in Leura. I'll take you walking in the Mountains sometime.'

I hate it when men do that, *I'll take you walking in the Mountains sometime.* Not would you like to go, or, we could go, but I'll take you. Big whoop.

Len

Stephanie probably preferred cabins to tents. I booked a cabin like the sleep-out at my Auntie's. Self-contained, with electricity and everything.

I hated the strangers in bed and breakfast places who demanded to know where you met and how long you'd been together and then demanded your address. Interfering hussies, trying to find out if this was your first time together, if one of you was married. They always knew someone who lived just down the road. I told Steph that if anyone asked, we'd been introduced by mutual friends. How long have you known each other? Not nearly long enough. Where do you come from? Sydney. Where in Sydney? Inner Sydney. This singles business was fucked. No wonder men gave up looking.

Stephanie

Probably Len didn't offer to pick me up because he didn't want to be seen with me. Kristy once started off a romantic holiday sitting in separate rows in a plane. Until then she thought the solicitor was a workaholic who was away a lot, had no idea he was married. I imagined consulting her in the middle of the night, the night before Len and I went to the mountains.

Don't assume anything. You can't be suspicious enough.'

Friday morning had a serious talk to myself. It was my own fault I hadn't asked him to stay over, my fault we weren't having breakfast together.

He was pacing around the tickets window at Country Trains Platforms when I arrived, just in time.

'I booked a cabin in the mountains.'

I was mad to go along with this myth that I was adventurous.

Katoomba looked like the set for a black and white film. On the platform hunched people in dark coats huddled under ancient black umbrellas. We walked from the brightness of the cafes into the fog. Tore the edge off my fingernail trying to convince the zipper of my parka to slot together at the bottom. Len walked on oblivious, head down, into the rain. I almost turned back to the station.

Airing the cabin might have gotten rid of the smell of mildew but fog pressed against the window, obscuring everything but a few blurry lights in the distance. Icy rain, fine and straight, soaked the deck. After Len said his Auntie had always made cocoa with honey and cinnamon, I made cocoa with his honey and cinnamon and crawled under the covers with him, the only cosy place.

Len

On Saturday Stephanie claimed her insides felt like bruised grapes. Maybe she hadn't done it since that husband of hers left, had a virgin's sensitivity. Kidding myself again. Probably slept around with her arty friends.

'I'll give you a massage instead.' Wasn't about to divulge how long it'd been since I'd been with a woman.

'But I was enjoying it, honestly. Just a bit out of practice.'

Rain drummed on the roof.

Stephanie

He brought me a bowl of cold cereal with heated milk. Malty and mushy. I reframed it into being served breakfast in bed. Better than being in a tent in this weather. Heaps better.

He rubbed the stubble on his chin.

'Toast? Vegemite? Honey? I'll get it. You stay warm. Sunday night, back in Sydney, if we haven't done all the walks on the list, you won't be too disappointed, will you?'

I promised not to hold the weather and missed walks against him. Honesty tasted good. He pulled his fleece jacket on. His legs were just tan enough so it looked like he was wearing pale bicycle shorts. He pulled on socks and track suit pants. The lights flickered. Thank goodness there were plenty of blankets and quilts. The city should have been scarier than the country but it never was.

Len

'The only reason I stopped bushwalking with Auntie,' I told Steph, 'was because I had this obsession that my birth mother might need me.' Currawongs called haunting messages across the valleys. 'Time to start looking for her. I thought it'd be easy. Just find the adoption agency and they'd introduce us.'

'That's how you found out Janet had been at a caravan park?'

'No, that came much much later. I gave up looking that time and joined my first bushwalking club instead. I was seventeen, young enough to think I could walk away from anything.'

Stephanie

It was still dark when I woke.

'No chance of boiling a billy in this weather.'

'My turn to make a cuppa.' I had to look for the switch on the electric jug. Same jug as the one in my counsellor's waiting room. *When have you been shown love that you didn't accept as love*, she'd asked over a year ago. When I was in kindergarten, my father used to shine my shoes and leave them outside my bedroom door. My mother said that was love. She cared about shiny shoes. I never even thanked him. Love was when someone did what I wanted them to. That Thermos, that bowl of mushy cereal, that billy can – they weren't supposed to show love, were they? I wanted to ask Len when he had been shown love that he didn't know was love, but it was too intimate a question. I didn't know him well enough.

Our footsteps echoed through the corridors of pubs, offices and industrial buildings around Katoomba Station that evening as we walked the wet streets searching for the right cafe. I stopped to look in a real estate window. Len said real estate was less than half the price it was in Sydney. Arty shops everywhere. I could almost afford to live here– pay half as much rent, teach a few classes, sell the occasional painting.

Len

A scrawny boy with hair smacked wet against his scalp was taping a MISSING FERRET sign to a telephone pole outside a cafe.

The boy's misery made me want to keep walking.

        PERMISSION TO LIE

'We can find something better,' I said, smelling roast chicken like my Auntie's, remembering the headlights of her Hillman emerging from the mist when she picked me up at the station.

Stephanie

We walked back to the cabin without needing umbrellas, pinprick stars puncturing the blackness.

But Sunday morning the fog obscured the landscape again. My hand itched to re-create textures I'd only glimpsed. Dark trunks of sinuous trees in art nouveau poses began to emerge. Len would know the names but I didn't ask.

Len

I couldn't wait to get moving. Did a few stretches, packed my backpack, hoping the fog would clear.

'Don't suppose you feel like a walk in the rain, Steph?'

'Um.'

'I could go for a quick one by myself?'

'I'm coming.'

Her walking shoes were pathetic. Dunlop Volleys. Soaking of course. Felt like giving her my talk on hiking boots.

I walked in front of her to watch for rock slides and fallen trees. Rivulets crossed the path, tumbled into waterfalls. I let her catch up, found a dry cave to eat lunch in.

Stephanie

He leaned into the slanting rain, waiting at each rock shelter, then a cave where I could pull back the hood of my dripping parka and share the sandwiches he'd packed, the steaming coffee. He gazed out at nothing.

'I don't suppose you've heard anything about your birth mother?'

Len

'Yeah. A letter and a photo. Janet's been dead sixteen years. Never married. Died the same year as my Kid Care Auntie. Both gone.' That photo showed a young woman in a plaid dress with big buttons, clutching a watering can, standing in front of a prunus. Her dark hair curled in the heat. In the background a sash window was partly obscured by a striped awning. Metallic glare bounced off the fender of a Hillman.

'When did you find out?'

'The night we got back from the valley. Too knocked about to call you. Didn't want my bad news spoiling things with you.' I felt like turning away when Stephanie's eyes traced around my face, as though she were drawing me. She touched my soaked sleeve. I covered her cold wet hand with mine. Through the fog I imagined the cliffs, radiant in the sunlight.

'Finally, I'm freed from searching. You okay? How's your painting been going?'

Stephanie

Back at the cabin, leaves on dark branches trembled open. I should have packed a sketch book, quill, ink, oil pastels. As the fog thinned, I saw tufts of mustard-coloured grass, the tangled snares of tree tops, the curves of long grasses, the zigzagged fronds. Clouds tumbled across a blue field like woolly animals. What would emerge after the white oil pastel marks were covered with dark ink would be subtle, like objects emerging from the fog.

Len

Showed Steph how to tell the ages of the male Satin Bowerbirds by their colouring. Urged her to have the first shower, in case the hot water ran out.

'Next time,' I assured her before we caught the train back, 'we'll have better weather.'

PERMISSION TO LIE

Before I finished wiping down the bathroom mirror with my towel it clouded up again. I stared through the beads of moisture, my hair curling in the steam. Remembered the photo. Her dark curls … that plaid dress with big buttons … her watering can … her prunus tree … the striped awning of her house…her car. I could smell the roast chicken.

Stephanie

Next time. I heard him say it.

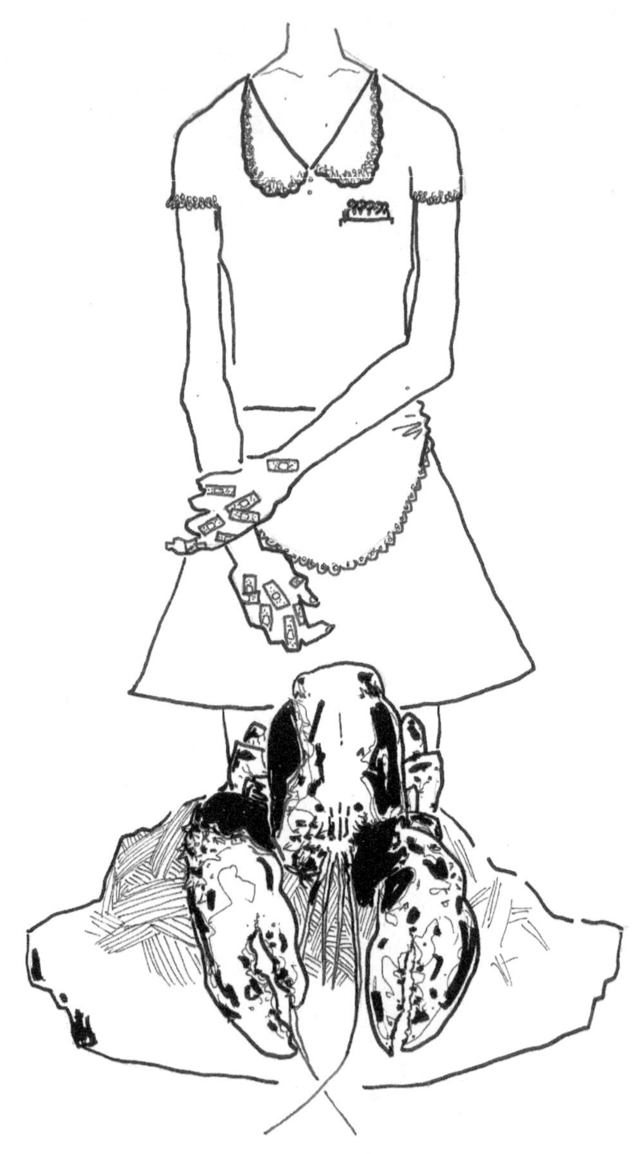

The executioner

Carefully I pry each Japanese beetle from the leaf of a tomato plant and drop it into a jar. Dad pays me a cent for each one I catch and drown in kerosene. But during the night the beetles come marching back with dozens more. Rows and rows of ugly brown beetles outlined in black, carrying away our tomatoes and corn. They're stealing, really. All summer I've had nightmares. The way they jaw their way through the tender leaves until only the tough stem and a network of veins are left. My hands stink of kerosene. I wash and wash but nothing gets rid of the stench.

This is the third noon in a row the red line in the thermometer has topped one hundred degrees on the back porch. The back of my legs are dented with the diagonal pattern of the wicker chair. Yesterday Carole and I were so bored of Cluedo that we set up the Monopoly board instead. Now she owns hotels on the Boardwalk and Park Place so the game might as well be over. At the real boardwalk, in Atlantic City, swimmers are keeping cool by bobbing up and down in the waves and every third shop sells salt water taffy. I used to think pregnant women went there because the salty air brought out *a lady's child* but Mom insists the song says *a lady's charm*. Then she told me I was too young to be concerning myself with childbirth. But I knew about it already. About the pain. Carole's Mom told us everything. And how it felt. She said that some things that really hurt turn out to be the best things that happen to you.

Carole and I can't listen to Queen for a Day on the radio at my house because Gramp is listening to the Dodgers lick the Yankees at full volume. He's lived in our house in New Jersey forever, since before there were Japanese beetles in his garden, since before I was born, but he's still loyal to Brooklyn. He says the beetles gradually crept up from the farms in south Jersey; I was picturing them zooming in, in formation from Pearl Harbour. My family just crossed the George Washington Bridge over the Hudson River. Mom hogs the television, watching Joe McCarthy being clever in court while the iced tea steeps. She's crazy about the Senator. I'm crazy about Mr Hardy, a teacher I had last year in seventh grade. Carole's crazy about Mooney, the new cashier at the supermarket. He came home from the Navy with tattoos. And goodness knows what else, Mom says.

Carole has to go home for lunch so we pack up boring Monopoly. I unpeel my shorts from the chair, put on my sandals and run across the road to see if Joni wants me to help entertain her twins. Angey will be working at his hot dog stand in Paterson. His real name is Angelo but he is really nice anyway. The real name for hot dogs is frankfurters but the sign at his stand definitely says hot dogs and they're oozing mustard and ketchup and pickle relish all at once. We don't eat hot dogs.

Joni comes to the door in pin curls and rollers. She lifts the glass coffee flask off the stove and flicks off the radio. Glory and Marietta are kneeling on kitchen chairs, staring out the back windows, into their yard. The curtains are drawn on the other windows and everything's shut tight. It's dark and, as Mom would say, close.

'You know, you're a doll to come over in all this heat? A living doll.'

For once the girls don't notice when Joni hands me a small red cardboard box shaped like a circus cage. There's a woven string handle so you can carry it like a purse if you go out. Animal crackers.

I march a parade of them up the Formica kitchen table. 'A lioness with a curly mane for Glory, a blonde tiger for Marietta, a spotty giraffe for me.' Pairs line up as though they are going to board an ark and I sing the 'two by two' song quietly so the girls'll come close to listen. Normally, by now they'd be climbing all over me, their arms around my neck, their hands tangling up my pony tail. Usually they can't wait to eat animal crackers. Off with their heads! they yell.

I walk over to the window to investigate. The yard isn't fenced. The wire dog-lead whines and screeches along a heavier wire. The noise so shrill it hurts. I watch Rusty race forward until she reaches the end, then spiral off the ground by her collar. She looks like she's a swinging car in a ride at Palisades Amusement Park, only she's swinging by her neck. She's drooling and her fur is matted and soaked; her face is covered in foam. She looks like she doesn't know where she is and an awful hoarse sound's coming out of her throat, like dry-retching. It's so scary I can't stop looking. Poor Miss Rusty.

'Heat stroke?' I ask Joni.

'Disgusting beast. Mad. I've already called the pound, twice.'

The girls are watching Rusty trying to bite through the wire. I try not to think what will happen if the wire breaks, and Rusty gets loose and runs all over the neighbourhood biting people. Finally the man from the pound backs his truck up their driveway. Joni asks me to take the girls into the living room. On Sundays their grandparents visit but the rest of the time the room is not used. I pack away the crackers so I don't drop any crumbs on the floral carpet. The girls are still glued to the window. I want to watch too. I need to learn how you calm down a mad dog. Joni puts some dolls onto the table under the crucifix.

'C'mon and play, girls.' she says.

'Do we have to?'

'You have to.'

'What's a pound?' asks Glory.

'What's a dog catcher?' asks Marietta.

I tell them what Mr Hardy would call a white lie: dog catchers find lost dogs and bring them home. Mr Hardy says sometimes people tell lies because they're trying to be kind, like when they don't want to upset someone. I try to distract the twins by making up stories about the objects in the glass-fronted cabinet but they are not interested, so we sing boisterous choruses of 'I've been working on the railroad.' I'm trying to think of a song to start next but all I can think of is, 'How much is that doggie in the window?' Then, at the last minute I remember; they like the one about the four-leafed clover. Mr Hardy says it's up to you to make your own luck.

We sing over the top of barking and yelling, some cracking and thumping noises. The door slams, and I sing even louder as the truck heads out of the drive. We don't stop until Joni comes back with four tiny glasses of Pepsi on a metallic tray. The ice creaks in the quiet as it settles.

'What's rabies?' asks Glory.

'Where'd you hear that?' asks Joni.

'From the man.'

'A pound of rabies?' asks Marietta.

'How many ice cubes are in your glass, Glory? One, two, three.'

'Four,' says Marietta.

'Well done.' Joni claps.

Mom read in *The Herald* that scientists dropped teeth in a glass of Pepsi and the Pepsi gobbled them up. I don't believe anyone would waste Pepsi doing anything so stupid.

'You've been a terrific help, doll,' Joni says. That means nap time. She slips something into my pocket as I drain the last few drops of diluted Pepsi into my mouth.

'I want to say good-night to Rusty first,' says Glory.

'Night Rusty, doll,' calls out Marietta as she rushes to the kitchen window.

'Where's Miss Rusty?'

'Rusty's gone to live on a farm where she'll have lots of other animals to play with and lots of space to run around.'

'When can we go visit her?' asks Glory.

'Nap time, twinnies!'

Both girls burst into tears.

My thumbnail bumps along the ridges and grooves on the edge of the fifty cent piece in my pocket. A week's worth of Japanese beetles. I walk up the street past the prickly hedge, and around the corner, to Carole's. Her mother's grey hair has been cut off straight at the bottom, like bangs. She's ripping strips from old clothes to make a braided rug and watching the McCarthy trial on television. All the windows are open but she's tied back the white curtains so the air can move around. Carole's bringing in the wash in case there's a storm. Roy Cohn has been named Chief Counsel, whatever that means. Carole's mother says he and Joe McCarthy are Fascists, and that Herbert Hoover is a Fascist, and that it's a crime the American people have sunk to this. I thought Hoover was the boss of the vacuum cleaner company, but he's not; he's the head of the FBI. Joe McCarthy's eyebrows aren't shaped like an upside down V like most people's. His start horizontal from his nose, then drop down at a forty-five degree angle until they end lower than the corners of his eyes. Joni sometimes sits in front of the window holding a mirror in her hand while she plucks hers. She tweezes until there are just two thin rows of hairs left and lots of puffy red skin which needs ice held on it before Angey gets home.

Carole's Mom says the Rosenbergs would still be alive if Roy Cohn hadn't been the Prosecutor.

'Dad says the electric chair is too good for spies.'

'You don't really think the Rosenbergs were spies do you? On that evidence?' Carole's Mom asks.

I don't know anything about the evidence but I remember the day last June when the Rosenbergs were given the chair. I think I heard the radio make the static-y zapping noise. Dad was driving to the lake and Mom was in the front seat. The sun was glaring in my eyes but I was so excited about going out in a motor boat that it's hard to remember exactly. I was calculating how much I had to save before I could buy a white bathing suit like the one I'd seen in a magazine. Dad thinks all spies should get the electric chair, not just the Rosenbergs, and coal miners who go on strike should be drafted into the Army, and if they won't go, they should get the chair. He said Ethel Rosenberg was such a tough bird that it took three shots of juice to kill her.

I wonder if Miss Rusty *is* at the farm. Three cracks, like gun shots.

'Human beings should never be electrocuted. Now we'll never know the real story.'

Sometimes Carole's Mom sounds just like a teacher.

It's even hotter outside when Carole and I walk along the curb, arms straight out at either side, like two fighter bombers. Despite having magic lotion to slick it down, Carole's hair is more flyaway than anyone's. We walk past the bend where the houses end, past stacks of empty cartons behind the hardware store, past the lane packed with trash cans, not stopping until we get to the corner of Rodney and Main Streets. During the school term a student in a white safety patrol belt is posted near the fire hydrant to help little kids cross the road but we're old enough to cross by ourselves, and anyway, it's summer vacation.

I yank open the heavy green door of the post office and hold it for Carole. No fan. No windows. Cigarette smoke hangs like spirals of blue flypaper in the heat. We can't even see if anyone is behind the grill where you line up if you want to buy stamps.

Pigeons coo on the roof while we inspect the fly-spotted black and white posters tacked to bulletin boards on the wall. No sense wasting time looking at the really old posters. Those criminals have crossed the Rio Grande to Mexico, or they're on death row, and no one has bothered to take their mug shots down. We inspect the clean new posters. Wanted. Dead or alive. Reward. Identifying marks. If we found a crook right under our noses, we could collect $2,000 and go to Atlantic City. All men. One has sticking out ears and is as jowly and fat as Joe McCarthy. He has a widow's peak too. McCarthy has a peak but he doesn't have a widow. At least not yet. He married his secretary, Jeannie, and they adopted a girl from an orphanage.

Carole's Mom thinks there's something queer about it, but it's nice actually. If you're adopted you know your parents really truly want you.

The smell of sugar cookies floats out the window of Mr Herr's apartment next to the Post Office. His door is propped open onto the sidewalk. Every day, just as the kids are coming home from school, he lifts a new batch from the oven of the kitchenette at the top of the stairs. We sign off our detective duties for the day.

'You hoo, Mr Hairless Herr,' says Carole.

'Hel-loooo.'

Carole wants to ask him where he got the tattoo on his arm. He tip toes down the stairs carrying a plate.

'Sweets for my sweeties.'

The top of one ear is torn like he's been in a dog fight. We reach forward to take a cookie without getting too close. Baldie Herr invites us upstairs to have a tea party with his talking crow. I've never seen a crow that can talk.

'Next time,' Carole says, nudging my ribs with her elbow.

The old man and I echo, 'Next time.' When he turns around I can see tiny indentations in the back of his skull.

We run across the train tracks near the supermarket to visit Mooney. I'm not going to waste my fifty cents on chewing gum. The guy Carole thinks is such a hunk smokes Lucky Strikes and looks like a grease-ball with the collar of his shirt flipped up. Joe McCarthy's voice drones on the supermarket radio. I point out that Mooney's long hair is parted on the same side as the man's in the poster but Carole covers my mouth with her hand.

'Hi Mooney,' she says.

'What have you girls been up to?'

'Nothing yet,' she giggles.

When I get a boyfriend from the Navy he won't stink of tobacco. He'll listen to the songs that make it into the Magic Circle on Make Believe Ballroom. He won't care two cents about Communism.

Carole says you have to expect someone from Paterson to be a grease. One pretty bridge over a river isn't enough. Mooney takes the bus six miles each way to work here. When we go to Paterson, Mom locks the car doors before we drive past the shopfronts with newspapers taped over their windows, and more shopfronts draped with purple rags where gypsies live. She says I have to wait until my sixteenth birthday before I can take the bus there by myself. A man wearing a Planters Peanut suit follows girls. Mom read about him in the local paper. When I'm sixteen I'm going there to buy a red skirt.

After dinner Drew Pearson's announcer voice sounds tired on the radio.

'Skip to the weather, thank you,' Mom tells him while she's washing the dishes.

'No wonder the man's exhausted, all the stuff he's done to try to destroy McCarthy and the Investigating Committee,' Dad says.

'Another day with temperatures over a century in the metropolitan area is predicted.' Mom snaps the radio off and I hear the first drops of rain.

Outdoors, in the light from the porch, the leaves bounce as they're pelted by raindrops. The shiny bronze beetles are probably hiding. Poor Miss Rusty. It wasn't her fault. She hadn't done anything. A thunderstorm is grumbling and rolling in. Mr Hardy says telling the truth is best even if it's hard and complicated. I don't think I'll catch beetles anymore. I take the fifty-cent piece out of my pocket and slide it into the slot in my bank. I hope Ethel Rosenberg and her husband are buried somewhere dry.

Courting the American tragedy

LAKE PLACID CLUB
SOFT BOILED EGGS

Place egg in the top of egg cooker. Ratchet
levers down to exact time, approximately
three minutes. Place two slices of bread
in conveyor. Cut each slice diagonally into
four identical triangles. Arrange around
egg cup. Serve with the LPC emblem
facing the guest.

Uncle had driven four hundred miles to pick me up from college
the day the semester ended. He had waited a long time to drive
me to Lake Placid where his boss was a member of the Club. I
do not exaggerate: when I was six weeks old, about to be named
after a Fifth Avenue truck, he'd promised my mother he'd get
me a summer job there when I turned eighteen.

The Club in upstate New York founded by the famous Melvil
Dewey, had been selected to be the site of the 1930-something
Winter Olympics. Uncle's boss raved about fireworks reflected
in a lake surrounded by mountains, tennis on clay courts, golf
lessons from pros, thousands of acres of God's own scenery. I'd
written my own application.

Uncle drove along the Lake before he pulled into the circular
driveway at the grand entrance to the Club. The Adirondack
Mountain air was crisp, sheer blue. We were so eager to explore
we ran up the steps between the imposing columns.

'Corinthian or Ionian?' he asked.

'Greek, anyway.' I was too excited to think straight.

The receptionist pointed around to the trade entrance and to the wooden tenement where I had been allocated a bed in a room with other waitresses. No key was necessary; the rooms didn't have locks. Uncle told me that wealthy people liked to rough it. Although the very elderly stayed in the hotel itself, most members stayed in wooden cabins. Like pioneers or frontiersmen. Like Abe Lincoln.

The dining room resembled a ballroom with high ceilings. After we admired it, Uncle left so I could get ready to work. Serving three meals a day, seven days a week for thirteen weeks sounded formidable but I might get a few days break in the middle of the summer.

The maitre d' walked up and down the lines inspecting the dining room staff.

'Hands,' he said when he stopped in front of me. I held them out, wishing I hadn't gnawed my nails.

Then, 'Get rid of the nicotine stains.'

'Turn around,' he barked at the next waitress. He ran his fingernail down the back of her legs. 'Step aside.'

The skirts of our uniforms were so long I don't know how he could have seen much of her legs.

Irma, the head waitress, told me later, 'Paint-on suntan and seams drawn with eyeliner pencil don't cut the mustard at the Club.'

Plump and powdery with faded split ends, who was she to talk?

I began by waitressing the Purina Chows conference. Dog food and cereal salesmen. Gross. On the first morning I served an old man wearing a checkerboard peaked cap, sitting across from a racy tart wearing fur to breakfast in summer. She looked decades younger.

'Poopsie, you like yer coffee with milk and sugar, do you?' he asked.

I tripped and splashed orange juice into his lap. Incompetence and nerves. Assuming daddy would know how mommy

                                    PERMISSION TO LIE

took her coffee. Oh my. I blushed strawberry pink every time one of the salesmen said something sexy, then grabbed me and squeezed.

'Roll with it, hon, it's all about the tips,' Irma said.

Roll with it? Honey roll over and lettuce on top? With a dog-food salesman? Just because I was waitressing, temporarily, didn't mean I couldn't afford to be a snob. Maybe I needed a flashy engagement ring so I could say, 'My man, he ripped the arms right off of this guy.' Nah. In desperation I invented a lifeguard fiancé, arriving in a week.

After breakfast shift on my nineteenth birthday, just like every other week day, I took my dirty uniform over to the laundry, picked up a clean one and carried it upstairs, hung it from a rafter. I slept until it was time to serve lunch. Afterwards I walked down into town and bought an engagement ring at the five and dime and had a birthday slice of angel cake.

Each time a conference left, the history of my waitressing mistakes disappeared with them. How were the Rotarians who were arriving for the next five days to know I'd never waitressed before? Or the Lions? Or the Masons? I practised new ways to earn tips. Each Sunday a special white uniform meant another fresh start.

After the conferences finished, the banquet tables were rearranged into stations and summer guests started arriving. My station, seven tables, could seat twenty-eight Club members and their guests. The professional waitresses, who worked Lake Placid in the summer and St Augustine, Florida, in the winter, started with twenty-eight guests a week. I was allocated only seven. If I failed one more subject at uni, I'd have to fly south with the professionals and wait on retirees and geriatrics in Florida.

Mabel, her walking sticks, and Dolores, her paid companion, occupied a table for six the whole summer. They showed me a postcard of the pink hotel behind a curve of palm trees where they spent winters. To fill in time between the resort seasons, they took an autumn and a spring cruise. Mabel tipped five dollars a week for herself, plus two for Dolores. As though Dolores was only forty percent human. Dolores was too busy batting her eyelashes at everything that wore pants to notice. The professional waitresses would have complained about Mabel's stinginess, but she didn't want them to wait on her anyway. She was a one-person charitable institution, helping needy Anglo-Saxon students work their way through college.

I was paid twelve dollars per guest from the Club, but had to give some of my tips to Sammy, the busboy who helped clear the tables and load the dishwashers. Neither of us was making enough money to pay tuition but he got off easier. No one cared how sloppily he stacked and carried dirty dishes, and no one inspected his fingernails or pinched his bum.

During exam week I'd stayed up all night to read *L'Etranger, The Outsider,* when I should have been cramming. Passion about anything not on the syllabus was cool, and I identified with Mersault squinting into the glare on the too hot, too bright beach, then smoking alone over his mother's dead body. Another misfit. At the Club I covered whatever I was reading with brown paper. No sense trying to discuss existentialism with people who painted their legs orange.

One day a week – Club rules – the menu was printed in weird spelling.

LPC

Poted beef with noodles or Steamed rys

Hadok with Parsli

Masht potato with Butr

Letis

Ys cream

Cofi

Dolores arrived at breakfast alone, jaunty and talkative. She filled me in about Melvil Dewey.

'M-e-l-v-i-l D-u-i as in the Dewey Decimal System,' she said, 'you college students would be familiar with that, well, the old goat also had a spelling system.'

To ensure the Club members received social, cultural and spiritual enrichment, that nut case Dewey built a library and banned alcohol, cigars, gambling, and keeping late hours. Thanks a lot. I pocketed a copy of the funny menu to show Sammy later. I had to fess up that my fiancé didn't exist. Dolores had the morning off to visit the chiropodist and hairdresser. She hoped I'd humour Mabel by letting her paint my portrait. The hell I would.

NORTH COUNTRY MAPLE WAFFLES

Butter at room temperature. Warm maple syrup. Add pecan crumbs to standard waffle batter. Cream half maple syrup into butter. Place scoop of maple butter in the middle of waffle the size of dinner plate. Pour remaining syrup over top.

To make up for my refusal to even discuss sitting for my portrait, I had to serve Mabel her Maple Waffles as a main course, instead of making her wait until dessert like everyone else.

Every Friday she forgot about her passion for down-home cooking and ordered 'lobster, freshly picked from the shell.'

In the kitchen I belted out, 'One picked lobster, hold the salad.'

'Honey, that f'in' lobster is wholly your problem,' said Grainer.

Every Friday as well as the battle of role demarcation with Grainer, I had an industrial battle with a lobster. I extracted meat from the tail and even the thinnest claws then plastered band-aids on my fingers. It was after Friday lunch that Mabel issued tips in pink-scented envelopes.

'Because you college students work so hard,' she said.

I did. I did. But she never gave me a cent extra. George Orwell's *Down and Out in Paris and London* made perfect sense. Of course restaurant staff spat in food before they served it. When I gave Sammy his share of the tips, he handed me a note, *All shud see the butiful after-glo on mountains to the east just befor sunset. Fyn vu from Golfhous porch.*

'You wrote this?'

'Melvil did. Want to go watch the Fourth of July Fireworks?'

Lake Placid
Creamed Chipped Beef on Toast

Make white sauce.
Stir in packet of chipped beef.
Serve warm on trimmed toast
triangles.

Dinner in the staff cafeteria (no sunset *vu*) was served from five-thirty until six. Wilted salads, discoloured chiffon puddings, reheated leftovers suitable for those without their own teeth. Day-old white bread that made a *whoosh* sound when you bit into it. I smelled but never saw steak. Grainer and the other chefs ate separately.

My shoulders ached from lugging heavy trays. My arms ached from carrying two stacks of four dinners each, the plates held apart by silver-coloured banquet rings. My fingers were burnt and cracked from grabbing hot china from the stainless steel counters before another waitress stole my orders.

'Don't smear blood on my plates,' roared Grainer.

I was scared of him.

'Occupational hazards,' said Irma.

The oak tray stand backed onto a two-storey column. The maitre d' regularly scolded me for leaning against it. I laced my shoes loosely. If only I could steep my blistered and swollen feet in a tub of ice water.

After dinner Sammy loaded dishwashers while I tipped the silverware into a wooden box in the scullery, dunked a bristled brush in Tarn-nix and scrubbed. Tarnished fork prongs cost jobs. No more nicotine stains. Instead my grey, shrivelled hands stunk of ammonia. I buffed each implement dry and re-set the tables, before sneaking into the compulsory evening lecture, late.

The lectures were another of Dewey's wacky ideas. Sometimes it was just a tennis player or golf champion trying to keep the hotel guests awake with funny stories. The night the President of the International Red Cross showed slides of his trip to Brussels, the kitchen boys borrowed cars, and Sammy and I snuck out to the Dew Drop Inn for Brandy Alexanders. I was sick of sucking up for miserly tips. Sick of holding my tongue when Mabel pronounced some right wing idiot a brilliant elder statesman from a fine old Southern family. At the Dew Drop, did tears run down my cheeks because of too much smoke, too much booze, or was it because my job sucked?

I didn't know until Dolores told me that the LPC was restricted, that Jews were banned along with booze and cigars. She asked me if Sammy were Jewish. How would I know? Did short and stocky with a bulldog jaw indicate Jewish? I was afraid someone would snitch on him. We gave up attending the lectures, and drinking at the Dew Drop, for the privacy of picnic nights at Cascade Lake five miles away.

Crisp nights I lay on my blanket on the grass, listening to the babble of the stream and love-making, the thunk of a knife slicing stolen watermelon, the sizzle of stolen steaks on the log fire. Cascade Mountain and the pine trees grew darker until the night sky became thick with stars, some green and shooting to somewhere far away.

The moonlight was brilliant. Dozens of college students comatose as geriatrics. Just enough energy to raise the hand that held the beer. Just enough energy to lie there while Sammy made love to me. Not enough energy to nag him to buy more condoms. Not enough to walk into the town during the day to buy new shoes. Not enough energy to read *No Exit*. I crossed my fingers I hadn't flunked out.

LAKE PLACID SURPRISE

Peel cantaloupe from top to bottom. Slice
one end. Stand melon on flat end and cut
off top. With a spoon scoop out and discard
seeds. Invert melon on a rack to drain.
Make a packet of red Jell-o, (alternate
weeks use green Jell-o) following directions
on box. Turn the melon right side up.

Pour jelly into melon. Cool in refrigerator
until set. Cut into smiley wedges. Serve
jelly side up.

I elbowed aside a professional waitress trying to worm in ahead of me in the breakfast pick-up queue. Surely my period would resume when life returned to normal. Eggs over easy; next to, not on top of, one and a half slices of medium toast. Bacon with all the fat trimmed, leave the fat on the side. One grilled tomato half, skin removed (hold the cheese). Nauseating.

A New York City lawyer who sat at one of my tables kept turning around. Irma was standing right there rearranging vases and Sammy was away setting up buffet lunch at the Golf House. Who was there to look at? As the summer progressed, fewer and fewer guests bothered to get up in time for breakfast. The lawyer asked if he could take me rowing on Lake Placid. I couldn't admit to a fifty-year-old man wearing Brooks Brothers casuals (Dolores told me) that I usually took a nap. I met him outside the Lakeside Clubhouse, my bathing suit covered by a summer dress. Poor Roberta, the farm girl who worked in a factory in Dreiser's *The American Tragedy*. She was tipped out of a boat and drowned in a lake here in Godzone, Upstate New York. The boss's nephew, who made her pregnant, didn't want to marry her.

The lawyer rowed facing the birches and mountains, his back to me. Sometimes he turned sideways to ask questions over his shoulder. Was I majoring in political science? Thinking of law school? Would I like to meet his lawyer sister? Their NYC firm employed paralegals. He was courteous, not like the Purina Chow hounds. He rowed back to the boathouse and gave me his business card. Just enough time for me to change into my uniform and serve lunch, not enough time for me to answer his many questions about Sammy.

GRAINER'S PINK GRAPEFRUIT ENTREE

Cut grapefruit in half along equator. Cut around each segment with grapefruit knife. Place whole maraschino cherry in centre of each half. Drizzle clover honey and maraschino juice. Place under broiler for two minutes.

Sammy promised he wouldn't make me pregnant. We used condoms two days each month. If by some weird mistake it happened, we'd keep the baby, he said.

'Pug-nosed cuties,' he said. 'I'm going to be a vet. My parents would help.'

He didn't mention my degree. Or my career, whatever that might be.

Irma would know where to get an abortion but I couldn't bring myself to bother her. She was always leaving the dining room for the foyer because of hot flushes. I sneaked into the toilet dozens of times a day to check whether The Curse had arrived, making deals with Mother Nature that if I were spared, I'd never refer to it as The Curse again, but welcome My Friend, if only I could be spared this one little pregnancy, if that's what it was. If only I could be spared telling my parents; and Uncle. Oh my God! His boss. And Granny. The whole question was too humiliating to contemplate.

Within five minutes of finding out I would not have to marry Sammy or seduce the balding lawyer who probably preferred Sammy, Irma winked. It had to be a coincidence. The temperature dropped and my enrolment forms arrived in the mail. Grainer said he hoped I'd return next summer. College began in a week. Before serving dinner I went up to Dewey's library to look for a copy of *On the Road*.

The library is a social institution

Bad luck you catch your heel in the Boston cobblestones and yank it clean off on the way to your first full-time job. You're clutching that heel like a frozen talisman as you mount the steps of the weathered brick building that first morning.

The edge of a woman's mauve coat drags in the snow on the steps as she bends to pick up a newspaper. She rounds up, stares at you.

'Whatever possessed you to wear heels in this weather?'

You look at the woman's clunky snow boots. She hollers for someone in the library to bring out a hammer for your shoe, and a bucket of salt to dissolve the ice on the steps. Heels are weapons. You need them to step back on the insteps of the men who rub their dicks against your bum on crowded trains, but you can't be bothered trying to explain that to someone her age. She hands you the hammer and you lean against a column to whack the heel onto the protruding nails.

'You are … ?' She scrutinises you again.

'Allegra. The new …'

'From Copley Square?'

' … Young Adults Trainee.'

'Of course I received the letter from personnel, but was expecting … from your pretty name … a petite person.'

She stands between you and the double doors and announces she is Lavinia N. Pinsky, The Librarian. She removes a glove and extends a pale hand, 'And you, Allegra, are late.'

You've only lived in Cambridge a few months. When you get to know the MTA system better you'll arrive on time. Helping poor kids get an education; that's the important thing.

The Librarian leads you into the foyer, wrestling one arm out of the sleeve of her coat as she turns toward the woman who brought the hammer. 'Josephine, the Adults' Librarian, meet Allegra, the new …'

Josephine holds the shoulders of the mauve coat while The Librarian withdraws her other arm. She reclaims her coat and asks Josephine whether she's wearing a new waistcoat for a special occasion. Josephine is wearing a maroon waistcoat in honour of your first day. She winks through gold-rimmed glasses as she tweaks one of the plump curls on her forehead.

On your right under the high dome is the circulation desk. Josephine points out the obvious – the Librarian's Office, the Young Adults' area, and the toilet. Light attempts to sieve through grimy windows. The Children's Room and Staff Room are straight ahead; Adults' and Reference to the left.

Mrs Pinsky asks her to show you how to open the desk. As the boss flips a light switch with her left hand; light winks from her diamond rings. Josephine marches around to enter the horseshoe desk. Your fingers accidentally bump when she hands over the list of tasks.

'We don't set the date stamps with tweezers anymore, thank goodness, just break our nails yanking around these wheels. See? February … 5 … 1962. Easy.'

You wonder how long you'd have to work here to ignore the insect wings, reinforcements and chewing gum wrappers trapped under the typewriter keys.

'Two, count the coins into the change drawer. I'm happy to be your witness anytime you're handling money, my dear.'

Back home you'd balanced the supermarket take every Saturday and your boss never called you his *dear*. Now you're being shown how to enter yesterday's circulation and told you work Wednesdays from one till nine and other days from nine till five. Any idiot can read a roster.

Your mother thinks no one will marry you if you're too educated. You haven't told her about the library science masters you have to begin to keep the traineeship. The first course is The Library is a Social Institution, then Cataloguing.

A patron waddles toward the desk with her hand extended. Your first customer reeks like a subway recess. Quickly you hand over the key. When she comes out of the toilet, she tosses the key on the counter. Its jangle propels Mrs Pinsky from her office.

'Don't give her the ding-a-ling in future.'

'The ding-a-ling?'

'The ding-a-ling what'zit.'

'The key? Why not?'

'You'll soon recognise the no-hopers who come in just to warm up and take advantage of the amenities.'

You ask if the roster is wrong. Surely you're supposed to work the hours that the kids aren't in school. She waggles her head, no, and returns to her office muttering that you have a thing about youth.

The man in the wool beanie wants help to look up wars in the card catalogue. You ask if he is interested in a particular battle.

'Not wars!' He draws air circles over his chest and lowers his voice, 'Who-res.'

You stay cool, tell him there are cards for authors and titles as well as subjects. Mrs Pinsky orders you back to the desk and tells you not to hand him the what'zit. He rolls his eyes. As soon as she re-enters her office he gestures toward the toilet. You hand over the key. In the Young Adults' section, cartons from the main library's promotion, *Asian Adventure,* cover your desk. The screech of ripping sticky tape coincides with the creak of Mrs Pinsky's office door.

'Ching-chong,' the boss tilts her head from side to side as she flits past, a turquoise silk scarf floating behind her.

Josephine comes over to invite you out after work on Friday. She knows a little place below street level in Chinatown that does the best fried shrimp on toast. You have no plans for

Friday, but in no time you'll have friends your own age and it could be hard to let someone older down once a pattern is established.

At morning tea she says a children's assistant named Carlie will be starting soon. Carlie doesn't look like someone who topped her year at Wellesley, whatever that means. Before you have a chance to find out which year, Josephine wets her lips and tells you you're sitting in Lavinia's chair and that the cup decorated with peonies is the boss's special cup. Who wouldn't use the thinnest, prettiest cup? Mrs Pinsky can get stuffed.

You're stapling a red background for the new posters when Mrs Pinsky shrieks from her office to use thumbtacks instead of staples, and not red.

You step down from the chair and walk over to her door. No sense in mimicking bad manners. She believes the properties of the colour red excite immature people. You step back on the chair. Whack. Another staple attaches red paper to corkboard. Whack.

The circulation statistics plunge. From her office Mrs Pinsky demands the date you commenced duties. Bernadette, the teachers college student who comes in to shelve books, gives you a sympathetic look.

A chance to break the routine of clerical work and ordering from pre-approved book lists arrives in March – a note inviting you to start giving book talks at the Yellow House.

Josephine, who has been avoiding you since you saw her smirking as she handed Carlie a cup of tea in the peony cup, says the Yellow House is where unwed pregnant girls wait to have their babies. Taking books to the girls will boost the circulation.

Josephine says they'll only read escapist crap and hands you science fiction by Heinlein and Asimov. Mrs Pinsky floats past, plucks them from the box and drops in *Gone with the Wind*.

Bernadette replaces Scarlett and Rhett with high school texts. The cleaner, unasked, leaves rumpled copies of *The Watchtower*.

You avoid books about adoption, failed relationships and names because the girls have to hand over their babies without even giving them a cuddle. Eventually you tip all the books out of the box.

Although you sit on the steps of Widener Library licking ice cream cones with ridiculous jimmies sprinkled on them, and hang around the Harvard Coop, Albinoni's and the Square, no Harvard or MIT student asks you out for a cup of coffee, much less a beer. The weirdos on the subways don't count. You spend Saturday nights reading *Catch-22*.

The Radcliffe graduate in the apartment across the hall thinks it's a joke to be on the shelf, hilarious to have a BA next to her name, but no MRS. Together you send away for tickets to see *West Side Story*.

Visiting The Yellow House has to be rescheduled because of another holy day. The card catalogue has no information about contraception. The girls would have no hope of getting a diaphragm or condoms in Massachusetts, and they'd have to marry a doctor to get the new pill.

You stare at the photographs of couples having Asian adventures. The hands of the clock move so slowly you could practically get to the travel agent and back between ticks. 1:51 the Greek Isles. 1:57 Bali. 2:03 Paris. Books on touch typing and Gregg shorthand go into the box. *The Diary of Anne Frank*. 2:10 Amsterdam. Being confined to an attic didn't prevent Anne from falling in love. *To Kill a Mockingbird?* Definitely. And *The Catcher in the Rye*. You'd almost wrecked the job interview arguing about who should be allowed to read it. If you're old enough to go through childbirth and have your baby snatched away, you're old enough to read about Holden

Caulfield. Bernadette pretends not to read *Mademoiselle* during her breaks so you include a copy. At the bottom of the box you sneak in knitting wool, needles and layette patterns. You'd knit everything in pure white if an angel baby were going to fly out of your arms.

'I didn't think I'd have any trouble with you, you look so solid, Allegra, but The Monsignor from the Diocese has complained.'

You ignore her crack about size. He didn't seem to think you were disrespectful yesterday when he eavesdropped the entire afternoon. It isn't your fault if The Monsignor doesn't want the tough, cigarette smoking, gum chewing girls to knit booties with the soft wool you bought with your own money. So what if she sends Carlie next time. You turn away so she can't see how much you mind. She gives you permission to call her Lavinia.

It's impossible to excite a disadvantaged young person about learning if you rarely see one. Teenagers just don't find this stuffy dump attractive. But one afternoon dozens of them arrive to do assignments on the Battle of Dorchester Heights. There is no entry in the encyclopaedias. You're desperately checking the indices of books on the American Revolution, wondering if the students have invented a battle to tease you when Josephine waves creased roneoed sheets. Boston has a public holiday to celebrate this obscure battle which occurred on March 17th, St Patrick's Day, the day of the big parade. This makes sense.

You ignore her crack about size. The locals start to wear green every day. Even the dummies in the department store windows wear green the week before the holiday. Josephine suggests you leave your orange jacket in Cambridge if you don't want to be beaten up.

As you fall asleep and wake up you wonder if you appear brash. The Monsignor called you insensitive, but knitting booties was a sweet idea. You folded and refolded that afternoon. Should you have ignored their pregnancies, and just chosen the books other teenagers liked? If you hadn't been so headstrong you'd have taken the science fiction and romances Josephine and Lavinia suggested. Stubborn, just like your father, your mother always said. You wished you could redo the visit.

One blotchy fifteen-year-old, six months gone, whispered *ya'all* through uneven teeth. If she could find a lover, surely you could. In her place, you would get married so you could keep the baby.

At lunch Carlie, the Children's Assistant, sits alone in the staffroom. She puts down her pen and blows her nose, pushes aside Robert Lowell's poetry, a newspaper and the tissue box before sounding off about what a bitch Lavinia is. Apparently she barged in and threw a signet ring that ricocheted off the shelf and hit Carlie's lip. The evidence is there; Carlie's lip, already stretched glossy and smooth, seems to be swelling as you watch. She presses it tenderly with her finger while you lever open an ice cube tray. She hands over the ring and points out the engraving inside.

'*Poppy xxx Peony*. What's that mean?'

'Poppy — that's Josephine — used to have romantic holidays in Europe with Peony, she taps the Peony cup — that's Lavinia — all summer, every summer. Cosy, eh?'

You're saving all your holiday leave to go away with the special man you'll meet any day now. You avoid Carlie's eyes when you hand her an ice cube wrapped in a handkerchief.

It is only natural you're restless in hay-fevered, wild-flowered May. You go along with it when a theology student assumes you attend church. You try to think *quaint* when he asks himself over on a Saturday night to paste quotations in his Bible, but it's not amusing when he leaves before dinner, taking your scissors and paste with him. You help a forlorn foreign student find the Harvard computer. Married. You could have fallen for the

PhD student in the Harvard cafeteria if he hadn't reeked of formaldehyde. Maybe you're too fussy, but you wonder what it would be like to sit close to him in the movies.

Bernadette checks that the staffroom door is closed and glances around before she asks if you've heard the weird news; Carlie is moving in with Josephine. Nobody'd told you Carlie had finally found a place.

'She's been looking for a room for weeks.'

'A lot more than a room!' Bernadette thought having a boyfriend heightened her powers of perception. Carlie loaned her Blake's poetry.

'She needs space for her books.'

Carlie invites you over for dinner before you all go hear Joan Baez sing in a coffee shop. Josephine's kitchen is lush with the smell of roast lamb, onions and rosemary. Carlie sets the antique table with silver and linen. Like home, except for the open copy of Sappho's poetry and a bookmark with, *Girl, you turn me on* scrawled under a cartoon light bulb. Josephine winks, 'I suppose roast lamb is your mother's favourite, my dear?'

It is too much to shift the gears of the borrowed VW, and read directions and road signs at the same time. Bernadette calls you Alley and rambles on about bog poor orphans in institutions when her job is to pay attention to the map. She'd like to hear cannibal jokes to keep her from becoming teary. The two of you have been trusted to take library books to the Cardinal's orphan asylum in the suburbs.

Two nuns show you around the mansion, show you the electric train room which had been a billiard room. Who would have thought young orphans would have stylish haircuts? They sprawl on big stuffed animals or sit on rocking horses while Bernadette reads them stories, but the older kids are more interested in their television programs than in your library books.

You attempt to retrace the old cow paths back to Boston but become lost. What's the matter with you? Lavinia only tolerates you because it makes her feel smart to have someone around who knows less than she does. You crashed with the mothers-to-be, the boys at the rabbinical seminary, and the orphans. You are not cut out to be a lesbian, and you have no desire to be an unwed mother. Despite twenty-three years of trying to get into the slogger's section of heaven you haven't helped a single slum kid succeed, and you aren't even going out with anyone.

'Alley, did you see the gears on those bikes? Those thick white blankets? Someone must have the guilts big time to spend so much money on orphans. And, Alley, who makes the Yellow House girls pregnant?'

You can be more honest away from the library, 'While the Catholic Church prohibits the use of contraceptives …'

'My mother says those men aren't called Father for nothing.'

'I'm not Catholic.'

'Josephine's screwing Carlie, isn't she? You and I are the only ones who aren't lesos.'

'Bernadette, I need to get back into the Yellow House so I can help those girls.'

'Help them have abortions?'

'Abortions? Hell, no.'

'You took knitting needles, didn't you?'

You wake in the night. Oh my God. Knitting needles. And doze. And wake. Knitting needles. Oh my God. Who did make the Yellow House girls pregnant? Why are the orphans rich? What's wrong with Carlie living with Josephine if they're happy? Even if Josephine is thirty years older? Will you ever get anything right? The hell with counting change. Buy a plane ticket.

Cylinder for a tree trunk

You could paper walls with the obituaries Mother has saved. Her desk is stuffed with yellowed birth notices, bridge scores, warranties and credit card statements. In amongst her insurance papers, snapshots and greeting cards there's a note from your niece. You probably shouldn't read it. *Thanks for giving me Louisa's painting, Grandma. She's so bold with colour. That fat wild man with the wobbly arms!* Obviously your feminist response to one of de Kooning's women was too big and bold for your mother and her faux colonial decor. Was your niece just being polite or did she really like your eccentric art? If Mother had told you she'd hated it, you'd have had it shipped back to New York, to the gallery.

Only one dour, tight landscape remains in Mother's over-heated apartment. Circa eighth grade. You lift it off the hook and wipe the dust off the top of the frame and lean it against the waste basket, ready for a long ride in a big truck, as she would say. Unless she wants it in the nursing home with her other cringe-worthy mementos. The slate blue wallpaper rectangle where it hung looks accusing.

Another obituary. For Frederick Mueller, your first art teacher. Married forty-six years and still living at the same address.

More than anything, when you were a child, you had wanted to draw and paint, but Mother felt you needed ballet lessons. They failed to provide you with a graceful carriage, and hadn't stopped you from galumphing up and down the stairs and sliding down the banister. When she finally admitted to Dad that ballet lessons hadn't worked out the way she'd hoped, you pestered to do art instead. You were spearing meatballs one Friday night at dinner, when you overheard her telling Dad that you'd need a lift to art class the next morning.

Snow fell on the Ramapo Mountains that first Saturday when Dad backed the Chevy out of the garage. He drove past the giant rock dumped by a glacier as it receded back to Canada. You felt happy.

He drove across the train line, past suburban corners snowy as Utrillo's paintings of Montmartre but lacking their charm: the sweet-smelling bakery made of red bricks, the actuary's office with old-fashioned gold lettering on the window, the stucco post office, the Castle gas station.

It didn't take long to reach the housing development and the Muellers' yellow weatherboard house. Their front lawn had snow-topped shrubs, and a couple of saplings wrapped in three-sided burlap shelters.

At the door Mrs Mueller took your black boots and clacked the soles together over the iron railing, before she took them indoors and added them to the row standing on newspapers. She threw an Army blanket over the dining table, spread oil cloth over that and smoothed it with large rough hands. She covered the backs and seats of seven chairs with newspaper.

Mrs Mueller was big-boned, as Mother would say. Not delicate the way you expected a muse to look. Her brown hair was yanked back with the kind of elastic band that bound the celery at the fruit market.

When she took your hooded car coat she looked at the row of fasteners down the front. She looked at the cosy striped lining, and the label, then hung the coat up.

The house was cold. You wanted to huff out a breath to see it as a cloud, but managed to stop yourself. You'd never been inside an artist's house, although you'd seen pictures of Vincent Van Gogh's bedroom, of course. You expected sunny auras surrounding everything. You knew about artists.

'Frederick,' Mrs Mueller bellowed toward a room out the back, 'you'll be delighted to know the last of the young *artistes* has arrived. Don't forget to collect the money.'

Artistes. A good start. At eleven o'clock he entered the room and sat down at the table, rubbing his long thin fingers together to warm them before he separated a black and white photo from a page-a-week diary. A boring landscape in boring black and white. His brown eyes darted around, planning. He made pencil dots at regular intervals around the photograph, ruling grid lines on it while talking about how he was dividing the space into halves, quarters and eighths. Then, because you were new, he loaned you some pastels and helped you rule a rectangle in the middle of his pad of paper and mark the dots around.

'See the dot at the edge of the photo near where the branch touches? That corresponds to this dot on the paper.'

He watched to see if you caught on. You caught on. At school you reproduced masterpieces from the Metropolitan Museum. You'd choose a big pretend postage stamp to copy, the Angel of Peace or whatever. The art teacher took points off because you drew the perforations around the edge, like a frame. On your report card she wrote, *artists need not be rebellious.* You disagreed, then.

Now? Well, you haven't fought in any jungles or overturned any governments. You thought about the outlines of Hiroshima victims you'd inspired your own art students to paint on pavement at a nuclear disarmament protest. You still chuckle thinking of the look on the cops' faces. As you stood at the scene of the crime, mist became rain, and the permanent damage they were about to arrest you for dissolved into Ajax and water slops.

Mr Mueller retrieved a pencil out of his grey hair, sharpened it with his knife, and blocked in shapes on your page—a rectangle for the barn, a cone for the leaves on the tree in the foreground, a cylinder for the tree trunk, a square for the

PERMISSION TO LIE

background foliage, two arcs for the road leading to the bottom of the page. He worked his way around the table, blocking in the same landscape for each student. Didn't the others want to draw something exciting?

You can't help thinking about starting art school in New York. Mother had warned you that some of the other students would be the kind of people who injected heroin between their toes, but you didn't believe her. The scariest thing for you was walking into the studio to draw a nude model. Your palms were sweating and you'd given yourself a headache from nervousness by the time you unwrapped your charcoal and straddled a donkey. Then a man stepped onto the podium wearing a bubblegum pink feather boa, gloves, boots and a fedora, and everyone clapped and cheered. You only had time to draw one shoulder, arm and glove, but your headache disappeared.

Mr Mueller returned to you with a handwritten list of supplies to buy: paper with tooth, a box of thirty-six pastels, a kneadable eraser and an art gum eraser, a rolled stump for smudging. The students' portfolios contained drawings of muted snow-covered letterboxes, covered bridges, split rail fences, clouds and trees. Why have thirty-six glorious colours if you could never use them? You couldn't wait to get your hands on the pastels. You would keep the colours in the tray in perfect order forever: red, red-orange, deep cadmium orange, chrome orange, mid-cadmium, chrome yellow; the warm colours at one end and the cools at the other.

'Can we learn to draw horses?' The girl who asked about horses was snapping her pastels into pieces. In frustration, you thought.

'I think not.'

'Could I bring in some of Dad's photos to copy?' Dad and Mr Mueller belonged to the same Photography Club. Everyone in town knew Dad won third prize for his circus series. You'd draw the bored tiger batting the air with his paw: magenta, red-orange and chartreuse, sharp angles and zigzags.

'If we behave ourselves, in the spring we can ask Rhonda, Mrs Mueller, to cut some flowers from her garden for us to draw. A real still life.'

'Great,' you said. Behave ourselves? Artists weren't supposed to behave themselves. According to the books in the school library, when artists weren't shivering in a garret, or threatening to cut off an ear or sun baking beneath a coconut palm in paradise, they'd be drinking Chianti from raffia-covered bottles in cafes. You'd been saving birthday candles to start dripping wax on one of those bottles the minute you found one.

Mrs Mueller emerged from the kitchen, wiping her hands on her orange apron, 'Collected the money yet, Frederick?'

Mr Mueller stood up, 'That's enough.'

She turned towards you, 'Only in America do artists have to teach.'

'Go rest, Rhonda. I can take care of the refreshments.'

'His genius is acknowledged throughout Europe ...'

'Rhonda ...'

'... where he studied for six years.'

Had Mrs Mueller studied art as well? According to Mother, too much education made women peculiar, that's why the woman doctor in your neighbourhood had a mental breakdown.

The fridge door opened and closed. Glass hit metal. There was a gust of icy air after the back door banged shut. The muse had left the premises.

You didn't know what to do once you'd coloured in all the shapes in the proper colours. Around the table everyone had rectangular rust-coloured barns, conical dark green trees, cylindrical black trunks and branches. Identical, like on the wall in the primary school.

You broke the silence by asking Mr Mueller if you could borrow his white pastel. He looked at the finger marks on the edges of the paper, went into the kitchen and returned with a damp dishrag. While you wiped your hands he lifted the fingerprints from the page with the art gum eraser, collecting the crumbs in his hand. You asked what kind of artist he was.

'One that's not good enough.'

You asked what kind of art he did.

'Commercial, but not commercial enough.'

Everyone listened.

'Compromised,' he said, with a look, as though you might be too young to understand.

He went into the kitchen and returned with glasses of water and six cookies on a tray, informing us that pastel number 127, a blacky-green, was essential for landscapes with pine trees. We took turns using his. Next time we would draw tree trunks in autumn.

Mrs Mueller flung open the front door and traipsed across the rug in snow-covered rubber boots, lugging her wicker laundry basket into the kitchen. Tract houses were built on cement slabs and didn't have basements for drying clothes like the houses in the older parts of town.

'The money, Frederick. And don't accept any excuses this time.'

Dad had paid for the whole term in advance. Mr Mueller held his thumb and middle finger in front of his temples and ran them back through his hair which immediately flopped back on his forehead. He withdrew a different pencil from his hair and made your trunks and branches appear more rounded. Then he picked up a rust pastel and made a few twists on some lines sticking out of the snow. Dried leaves! He unscrewed his Exact-o knife and, with the fresh blade, cut a rectangle in the middle of six pieces of A2 to make mats and then stuck tape hinges on the top of each mat. He came around to you, secured the concealed hinges, and let the paper frame fall over the top of your landscape. Suddenly the drawing looked clean, framed and professional – too competent and slick for you to have drawn it and you hadn't, really, you hadn't. 'Finishing touches, that's all,' he shrugged as he stuck one end of a metal gadget in a bottle and the other in his mouth and blew a mist of Fixative. 'To keep the pastel from smudging. We'll let that set up a bit before you go. This week everyone take your drawings home. Let your parents see how well you're progressing.'

Mrs Mueller must have been heating baked beans in the kitchen, because the smell was warming the room as Dad's car pulled up.

By the end of a year in Mr Mueller's classes you'd learned that if you want to make a cylinder look rounded, one dark band down the middle is just as effective as two bands down the edges. Later, in art school, you were one of the few students who could draw. Of course by then, realism was dead and the fun had begun.

If you'd been there to stand over his coffin you might have advised Mr Mueller he shouldn't have been so eager to fix up students' work. 'You made me feel like I wasn't good enough,' you might have said. Sure there had been times when you'd drawn on a student's drawing to illustrate foreshortening, or how to turn a wrist. That wasn't the point. You fixed up drawings to teach, not so parents would continue to write cheques.

You put the annoying pastel landscape in the boot of Mother's car before you drove to the nursing home to visit, hoping she wouldn't want it and you could dump it in a bin.

'No', she said. 'I never particularly liked that one. But Fred Mueller told your Dad your art had a wild edge. He said your early work might be worth something one day.'

Seeing the jane

'Why are you sitting in the dark?' I flick the light switch as I open the front door.

'Been up the road.'

I walk straight through to the kitchen, dump the grocery bags on the table and rush to the toilet. When I return he's still trying to stand.

'Up the road? No wonder you're buggered.' I stow away the groceries we won't need tonight.

'*Was* buggered. I'm OK now.'

The thunder of water hitting the bottom of the kettle drowns his voice.

'You couldn't wait?' I kick off my heels, drag my arms out of my suit jacket and drape it over the back of a chair.

'Here, let me give you a hand.' He rises half way from his chair.

'Sit down. Rest. Just scrubbing the potatoes. You were all right, up the road?'

'All right. Didn't do the messages, but. Couldn't remember what we needed.'

The King of the Armchair trembles, turns in my direction as he sits again, hears the kettle whistle and waits to be asked if he'd like a cuppa. No need – one with milk, one without.

Tentative drops hit the tin kitchen roof, wobbly lines from the late dusk sky.

When the kettle is quiet, my father-in-law hears them.

'Good for the garden.'

When he'd knocked on my door six months after James died I'd hardly recognised him.

'You can put me up for bit? Can you, luv?' He dropped the worn suitcase held together by a leather strap at my feet. 'I remember you were a dab hand with the kettle and oven at my place.'

It'd been a decade since James and I had visited my father-in-law in Auckland. I didn't know him well enough to call him *Dad* back then. Within hours I'd settled him into the room I'd once planned to use as a nursery and hung a load of his clothes on the line.

He tells me again he wants to clear the gutters. James's gutters. Haven't been cleared in years. When James was alive, sheets of rain never flowed down the back wall. Dad's too frail to climb ladders, too proud to let me, and I'm too hard up to hire someone.

I wonder how I'll cope with the frustration of being unable to do things. In my thirties I'd gone to a costume party where a woman dressed as a grotesque infant lay in a huge basket. A note pinned on her bib with a nappy pin had said, NINA. I filled Nina's bottle, pulled her socks up and retied the ribbons that were supposed to hold them in place. When I left, Nina's eyes were closed and the fist on her pillow was clenched. All these years I've been curious why she didn't come to the party dressed as something glamorous like the rest of us. I can't imagine why anyone would choose to be helpless.

When hard straight lines of rain are shattering on the tin roof I remember the laundry and rush down into the yard, turning my face as I grab at the wash. I drape the damp clothing on the banister and the backs of chairs, and turn the kettle on again. When Dad's tea spills into the saucer, I pour it into the cup and hand it back.

'Ah, a nice hot cuppa. Thanks, luv.'

I ignore being called 'love'. He's outlived two wives as well as his son. Whatever I am, I am not his love.

I ask if lamb, peas and potatoes are OK. He always wants lamb and potatoes, preferably mashed potatoes.

'Lamb and peas and spuds – lovely on a wet night.' He smacks his lips, then straightens up. 'Mint sauce! That's the message I forgot.'

'I didn't forget your mint sauce.'

James used to plan what we'd eat. Seven menus repeated for ten weeks, the same meal each Monday night. I duplicated the lists, shopped and cooked because my time was less valuable. I looked forward to choosing from a menu on our birthdays and anniversary until we fell into the routine of returning to the local restaurant and always ordering onion soup and coq au vin.

'Quality assurance.' James used to sum up our celebrations.

Five business shirts, drip dried by Sunday night; sex on Wednesdays and Saturdays – he liked routines. I wonder whether he would have relaxed as he grew older or become more rigid.

Aw! Not pasta again? Our kid, if we'd had one, might have been more like me.

Six years ago, to celebrate the arrival of the tax refund in the mail, I had decided to surprise James by cooking *soupe à l'oignon gratinée* – a recipe so authentic I didn't know how to pronounce it. I made stock and sautéed the grated onions in butter. I traced around the rim of a tureen. The toast – rubbed with garlic – had to fill the shape to make the crust. When the fragrance of cognac was rising and the cheese covered crouton was golden, I lifted the tureen out and drew a ladle of hot liquid from under the crust, added a whisked egg and slipped the liquid back as though we shared a secret. I rocked the tureen gently and switched the setting to *bake*.

I changed my clothes, listening for James's key. At first I thought he'd missed the bus, or was caught up in a meeting, but he'd left at the usual time. I turned the oven down, remembering the night he'd driven dinner guests to Central Station and arrived back five hours later. They'd missed the last train so he'd decided to drive them all the way home to Katoomba. I washed the dishes and snapped the oven dial to *off*. Probably I was worrying over nothing this time too. I'd gone to so much trouble over that wretched soup! The cheese crust already looked leathery. How dare he not ring? I wondered if he might have gone for a drink with the new woman at work, someone he'd known at uni. I felt awful later, for being so quick to distrust him. I haven't tasted onion soup since.

Before I catch the bus to work, I usually set out a meat sandwich in a box, a hard-boiled egg or a piece of cheese, a piece of fruit, and two cups of hot milky tea with the saucers sitting on top. Dad manages the saucer-crowns easier than a Thermos flask.

Last week my neighbours phoned me at work when they found him sitting on the nature strip clinging to a telephone pole. That's twice he's had a turn. He gives the neighbours' kids money to buy him chocolate, then skips his tests.

'Everything OK, then?' I flick the grill on, and lower the potatoes into the boiling water.

'Everything's OK. The jane says I'm a remarkable specimen for my age, remarkable.' His chin wobbles.

'You *are* remarkable.' His cup and spoon teeter in the saucer.

'More remarkable if I didn't get so buggered.'

To say I hope I'm in as good shape when I'm eighty would be a lie. I'll be in far better nick; we'll all be in better nick. His generation went through both world wars and the Big Slump. My generation has had it easy.

With my feet up on a pile of newspapers on the coffee table, I slurp my tea. Before I was married I made this strong mug. Hefting it gives me pleasure. One fragile rattling teacup and saucer is enough.

'Why'd you need to see the doctor, Dad?'

'Just needed the jane to give me a repeat script.'

No new problem, thank goodness. We just manage with the diabetes and Parkinson's. I can't imagine how we'll cope when he gets worse. I move my feet. I can't think with my feet propped up on a table, can't think without leaning forward.

'I hate it when you call her the jane.'

'Just a word.'

'About gender.' My voice is too loud.

He leans forward and cups his hand around his better ear. 'About what?'

'Gender.'

James used to pride himself on his hearing. He'd help friends select their sound systems but miss my pleas for help with the cleaning, shopping and cooking. When we entertained, he made the coffee. Even the time I got so carried away with flambéing that I almost set the pass-through window on fire, they praised his dripped coffee instead of my Crêpes Normandy.

I could whisper my love when he was in cardiac intensive care and know by a ragged graph he had heard through the fog of unconsciousness. Blips of the heart ease communication with the unconscious. An unborn babe would have begun to hear my whispers while I became accustomed to the shape of the words in my mouth. Together we'd create the sounds and patterns of a language. By the time the babe was born the words would have lost their power to startle me. I could have started with *dear* and worked up to *love* and *darling*. Maybe by the time I was dropping the child off at school I'd be able to join the other mums in calling out, 'I love you,' as I returned to the car. I'd never managed to tell James when he could hear me.

Dad pulls himself up straight.

'And I say,' and he pauses, '*vive la différence!*'

When he smiles, leans back and stretches his arms wide, I see a glimpse of the charmer he must have been. I fetch a towel to mop up the tea.

'Words that put women down don't celebrate difference.'

He leans forward in his chair, his extended arm thrusting the agitated cup and saucer straight at me. I'm supposed to accept the saucer and put it on the table in front of him. God! I remember the chops. I grab his saucer, turn the chops, drain the potatoes and start mashing. I worry whether the mint sauce I bought is suitable for diabetics. I should make it myself. Tendrils of hot brown vinegar fumes would surround my face, curl my hair, like dyeing Easter eggs when I was little. You can make mint sauce by yourself but you can't dye Easter eggs without at least one child. I'd have to borrow one.

He likes his potatoes mashed with lashings of real butter and salt and parsley or chives, cream too if we have it. I worry about his cholesterol. Silly of me, at his age, with his infirmities. But James had high cholesterol and they are similar in so many other ways. I shove the pot in the oven to keep warm with the chops until he's ready.

'Thanks. Lovely cuppa, lovely.'

He wants another. His graciousness makes me feel rotten.

'There's more in the pot, Dad. Another cuppa?' It's not fair for me to pick fights with him just because he isn't my son or daughter.

'I was thinking, a wee drop.'

He means Scotch, not tea.

'Now, could I offer you one, m'dear?'

If I were kind, I'd have one, instead of wine. He doesn't mean any harm by calling me 'dear' and 'love' but people who use the words carelessly make it harder for people like me.

'Beloved.' I practiced saying it aloud once when the cat rubbed against my ankles. Then, 'Beloved Cat.' My lonely words of endearment bloom once a decade, after dark like an exotic flower, when someone is dead or dying. I pour the Scotch into the glass that's easiest for him to hold.

Whenever James took me to Auckland he and Dad went to Dad's local on Wednesday nights. The one time I was included, they abandoned me to go and get drinks. I was freezing when they came back from the men's bar an hour later, chortling and flushed, carrying two double Scotches and a Pimms N° 2 with lemonade. I'd never heard of a ladies' drink, and felt like a child.

Briefly, as the rain lashes the tin, Dad and I sit drinking together. He seldom mentions his dead wives or James but he must miss them, as well as his old friends. I dial New Zealand for him each weekend when the rates are cheapest. The shakes keep him from dialling as well as from writing.

'Who's your closest relative?' I asked when we were making the list of phone numbers.

'You are. You're my nest of kin.'

I heard *nest* although it's unlikely he said it. You are my nest. The sound of shelter, like a hymn. We are a nest. Together we nest, the two of us, unconnected by blood, sex or gender. Our family has atrophied to the point where we need a lending library for more than books. *I'd like to borrow one elderly veteran and one child for the long weekend please.*

After the stowing of the groceries, the cooking and the bringing in of the wash, after the rain, after the cuppa and Scotch, after our meal together and the washing up, I still haven't told him I'm going out tonight. At the last possible moment I offer him the morning paper instead of my company.

'Someone special?'

Is he hoping I've met someone or worried a lover might move in and push him out of the nest and into a nursing home?

'Just one of the men from work but we usually manage to have a laugh.'

I put on my raincoat and pick up my keys and wallet. I couldn't bring a lover home. Whenever anyone visited us overnight, James and I would hang a blanket on hooks over our bedroom door and spread another to muffle the noises that might escape under the door.

'Laugh? In this storm? Shall I wait up for you, m'dear?'

I decline, touched again that he's offered. Not having to come home to a dark empty house is enough.

By the time I get up on Saturday, Dad's already down in the yard, smelling the wet soil and worms, marvelling again at the architecture of the snail. As I hand him his cuppa, he hands me a bunch of parsley.

'Another healing day. Look, m'dear.' He takes a bulb of garlic from the pocket of his cardigan. 'Mauve, not bleached like the garlic in the shop up the road.'

I resented his intrusion when he first arrived. I didn't want to hear the toilet flushing in the night. I didn't want to have to do his dishes and peg out his clothes and bring them in again. I'd become accustomed to deciding what I felt like eating at the last minute and didn't feel like catering for his special diet. I sympathised with Goneril or Reagan evicting Lear and all his rowdy knights from her castle. I mourned the loss of my privacy and couldn't wait until some New Zealand cousin claimed him and took him back.

I tried to find an Anzac digger who'd come and visit. If he had a bloke to talk to he wouldn't talk to me about the Saida bints. *I don't care what happened on the Street of Whores in Port Said or Cairo or wherever it was! You can't call any Sydney woman a bint. Especially a doctor. And if you're going to live with me, you'll call her a woman or doctor, not a jane or bint!* I wasn't planning to say 'if you're going to live with me.' I didn't want to share my house; it just came out that way. I could just as easily have told him to leave. But he'd stayed calm when I lost it and I felt safe being honest. Eventually I stopped trying to change him.

My anger landed instead on my memory of James. So many liberated women had written books and not one word had sunk into his consciousness. My time would always have been less valuable than his.

I was ironing his shirt when he placed his coffee mug on my copy of *The Female Eunuch*. A coffee stain encircled the picture of the woman's body hung up like a garment.

The RSL said the remaining veterans were less spry than Dad – he had lied about his age to enlist – but perhaps he'd like to visit someone in a nursing home. Probably he would have, but the brotherhood of ex-warriors seemed more interested in the profits of poker machines than in assisting lonely Kiwis and didn't offer to drive or even phone.

'If you want privacy just tell me,' he said as I was going out. 'I don't want to be in the way of you bringing a bloke home.'

At my age. The woman who sits next to me at work says, 'If things get rough, just plonk him in a nursing home. It's not like having responsibility for a surly thirteen year old.'

I may play in my head with the possibility of discarding old men like broken toys, but I couldn't do it. When I think about Nina in the basket at that costume party I wonder if I wasn't needier than Dad when James died. I expected a baby to teach me to love, to give me permission to say simple words aloud.

'Dad, I need a hand. If you steady the ladder, I'll have a go at our gutters.'

Acknowledgements

Stories in this book have been published or broadcast, sometimes in slightly different versions, as follows:

Cherry Pie in *loose lips: UTS Anthology, 2004.* It was performed at the Sydney Writers' Festival in 2004

This Awful Brew in *The Best Australian Stories 2011,* Black Inc, 2011

Meant in *Antipodes 2010*

The library is a social institution in *Southerly, Little Disturbances, 2008*

A cylinder for a tree trunk in *Images, The Society of Women Writers NSW. Winner 2009 National Short Story Competition*

Seeing the jane in *Island 2007* and on ABC Radio National

For details about other
Spineless Wonders publications
go to:

www.shortaustralianstories.com.au

www.ingramcontent.com/pod-product-compliance
Lightning Source LLC
Chambersburg PA
CBHW050403110726
47899CB00008B/2626